FULLMETAL ALCHEMIST

The Valley of White Petals

Volume 3
The Valley of White Petals

MAKOTO INOUE

Original Concept by
HIROMU ARAKAWA

Translated by
Alexander O. Smith
with Rich Amtower

VIZ Media
San Francisco

FULLMETAL ALCHEMIST novel vol. 3
THE VALLEY OF WHITE PETALS
© 2004 Hiromu Arakawa, Makoto Inoue/SQUARE ENIX.
First published in Japan in 2004 by SQUARE ENIX CO., LTD.
English translation rights arranged with SQUARE ENIX CO.,
LTD. and VIZ Media, LLC.

Illustrations by Hiromu Arakawa
Cover design by Amy Martin
All rights reserved.

Published by
VIZ Media, LLC
295 Bay Street
San Francisco, CA 94133

www.viz.com

Printed in Canada

First printing, May 2006

Contents

The Valley of White Petals

Chapter One

The Colonel's Conspiracy

EVENING CREPT SLOWLY into the sky as the sun sank low over the rows of hills. In the east, the heavens had shifted from a dim blue to a soft crimson, then glowed bright red for the briefest of moments before drifting into purple. Here and there, the first stars began to twinkle.

"Night already . . ." muttered the boy Edward Elric, scowling at the glory of nature spread out above him. He squinted his eyes against the beautiful sunset. "How far is it to this town, anyway?" he shouted, shooting a withering glare at the setting sun.

His brother, Alphonse, turned and looked back at him. "Guess it's the wild outdoors for us tonight. That rocky outcropping over there doesn't look so bad."

Edward shook his head. "I'm tired . . ."

"Who wouldn't be, after walking the whole day in this wasteland. Come on. You can make it that far, at least."

It took more urging from Alphonse to goad his brother into a slow walk, each foot lifting and falling with an almost impossible slowness.

"Unh . . . I can barely move my feet." Edward dragged his feet in the sand, his gold eyes sparkling from under braided blond hair. His face carried the brightness of youth, but the hardness in his eyes and a right arm and left leg of auto-mail betrayed a past unusually difficult for someone his age.

The same held for his traveling companion, his younger brother, Alphonse. Alphonse should've been a young boy like Edward, but now he towered over his brother, a lumbering suit of metal surrounding the void where his body should have been. The only thing tying Alphonse's soul to the empty, walking suit of armor was a rune etched in blood on the inside.

Several years before, the brothers had broken the taboo of human alchemy, and paid dearly: Edward lost his arm and leg, and Alphonse, his entire body. It was a terrible weight to bear for two teenage boys. Yet they bore it all the same, without stumbling. Much.

Edward had joined the military. The day he became a State Alchemist, he and his brother burned down their own house, so they would never have a place to go back to. Together, they swore they would get back their original bodies someday.

Recovering a lost body was no easy task, and so they

traveled far and wide, gathering bits and pieces of information wherever they went, chasing down every stray rumor they came across. In fact, they should have been searching for a way to get back their original bodies right now.

But they weren't.

Edward scowled. There was a reason why they had to camp out here in the middle of this wasteland. "Darn it. This is all the colonel's fault."

"Well, this is as good a place as any," Alphonse said, ignoring him as he began to prepare the tent.

Edward slumped down next to the rock outcropping, pulled a dried hunk of bread out of his pack, and began gnawing on it, occasionally pausing to glare woefully at the horizon.

Out there, somewhere, was Roy Mustang, colonel at Eastern Command and the man responsible for sending them out into this wasteland in search of a town that might very well not exist.

"Why do we have to monitor this town anyway?"

"Now, now. The colonel's a busy man, you know. And we get it pretty easy as it is. We should cooperate when we can."

"Cooperate?" Edward shook his head, thinking back on the string of events that had led them to this desolate place. He clenched his fists and trembled. "We weren't cooperating—we were coerced!"

IT HAD BEGUN a few days before with two sudden words:

"No money."

"Huh?" Alphonse looked up. His brother sat before him, dumbfounded, his wallet open in his hand.

"I've got my wallet, but there's no money in it," Edward repeated, looking at the dishes stacked high on the table. The brothers were in a restaurant on Main Street in a small town. The restaurant itself was a hole-in-the-wall. In fact, the wall facing the road had been removed, so a number of the tables faced right out on the street. They had been eating there for quite a while.

"What do you mean, you don't have any money? This is a fine time to realize . . ." Alphonse trailed off, looking at the chicken bones picked clean, the flakes of bread on the tablecloth, and his brother. A small shred of lettuce hung from the corner of Edward's mouth as further damning evidence of the crime:

He had eaten a ton, and the bill on the table certainly showed it.

Alphonse leaned over the table and whispered, "Are you sure? You don't have any in your pocket?"

Edward silently nodded, searching his coat pockets and frowning. "This is bad. We've been eating pack food so long I hadn't checked my wallet."

Edward patted himself down, looking for small change.

For the last several days, the brothers had been deep in the mountains, chasing rumors of a book on human alchemy.

They had returned empty-handed, a great disappointment, but their resolve to get back their original bodies could not be broken so easily. Just sitting in a restaurant, eating real food and being around other people had done wonders to restore their spirits and strengthen their determination to try again.

"We'll find it next time, I know we will!"

"Yeah!"

The two had looked at each other, slapped fist over fist in a ritual gesture of shared purpose, and began talking about where they would go next. And then, Edward had pulled out his wallet.

"What are we going to do? I could've sworn I had some cash in here somewhere . . ."

Edward slid off his chair and opened his traveling trunk. He began rummaging through it noisily. The other customers watched, some curious, some simply irritated. Alphonse waved their glances away as if nothing was wrong.

"Ed . . ." Alphonse poked his brother, who now sat on the floor rummaging through his trunk. "I think it's a little obvious that you're searching for money. Everyone can see you. What if the waiters suspect something?"

"Suspect what?"

"I mean . . ." Alphonse hunched down as low as his massive frame would allow and whispered, "What if they think we're going to eat and run?"

"Eat . . . and run?"

Now that his brother mentioned it, Edward noticed the waiters and the cooks shooting suspicious glances their way.

"Uh-oh. They're on to us."

"Of course they are." Alphonse sighed deeply and looked down at his armor. "Look how grimy I am. We don't exactly look trustworthy."

Edward looked down at his own clothes. Living in the mountains for many days had left them soiled with dirt. Here and there, loose threads had snagged on bushes, fraying his jacket at the shoulders. "No kidding."

They *looked* like people without any money.

"There's a bank in this town, right? Why don't you go and—" Alphonse was about to suggest he go make a withdrawal when a dark shadow fell across the table.

"Hey!"

The brothers looked up in unison to see the head chef looming over them, a frying pan raised in his hand. "If you're planning on skipping out on the bill, I've got some bad news for you."

"N-no, sir! We'd never do that!" Alphonse blurted, waving his hands in hasty denial, but it was too late.

"Think you can fool me!? I thought you were eating too much. You've been planning this little caper since the moment you walked in here!"

"No, wait! Please!" Edward squealed. "We have money! I just have to get to a bank . . ."

"You think I believe a scruffy-lookin' kid like you's got money in the bank?!" The chef roared.

"Hey! Don't judge by appearances!"

The large man scowled. "How else am I supposed to judge you then, eh?"

"You have a point," Edward admitted.

"Guys, get out here!" shouted the man, sounding his frying pan with his fist like a gong. "We've got a couple of runners! Grab 'em!"

The other cooks came running out of the kitchen, bearing pots and pans and other implements of culinary destruction in their hands.

"We'll have you working for a month to pay this off!"

"No, wait! Al!"

Alphonse saw the look in his brother's eyes and nodded. They had to get their bodies back. They couldn't be stuck working here for a month. Edward dashed out the door, shouting as he ran, "I'm going to the bank!"

Times were tough; there probably were a lot of people who *would* eat and run, Edward thought. The restaurant was right to suspect . . . but that didn't mean they could waste a whole month working there!

"He's running! He's running!" the head chef shouted.

Alphonse waved his arms. "He'll bring money, really. Look, I'll stay here. Just wait, please! My brother's a lot more respectable than he looks, honest."

Alphonse shook his head. This was crazy. Who would

believe that the grimy, unwashed boy running down the street with a wild look in his eyes was a State Alchemist?

Leaving Alphonse behind to defend his honor, Edward ran at full speed to the local bank.

"Excuse me," he panted. "I'd like to take money out of my account!"

Edward flashed his State Alchemist's silver watch to the bank teller as proof of his identity.

"Now at least we can clear our name with the restaurant." Edward slumped down into a chair, wiping the sweat from his forehead. However, several minutes later the bank teller came back. "I'm sorry to inform you," he said curtly, "that Edward Elric's account has been closed."

Edward gaped.

"Please come again," the teller said cheerfully.

"Wait wait wait! I still have plenty of research money in there, I know it!"

"I'm sorry, but I can't confirm the details from this branch . . ." the teller repeated, showing Edward the door.

"Why not!?" Edward shouted. "This is a bank, isn't it? If I go back there empty-handed, that crazy chef's going to think we really did plan to skip out on the bill! This is . . . This is some kind of conspiracy!"

It was, in fact, starting to stink of more than just bad luck.

Edward left the bank, ran to the nearest phone, called

accounting at Eastern Command, and shouted at them about the trouble at the bank.

There was a click and then ringing. The person in accounting had abruptly forwarded his call without telling him.

"H-huh? Hello? Hello!? Who is this? Who am I talking to!?"

There was a brief burst of static, followed by the sound of someone picking up the receiver on the other end. Edward opened his mouth to shout again, but when he heard the voice on the other side, his face curdled into a frown.

"Long time, no talk, Edward."

"Hello, Colonel Mustang."

Roy Mustang was the officer in charge at Eastern Command. With his jet black hair and sparkling black eyes, Roy was the youngest man in military history ever to have reached the rank of colonel, and he was a State Alchemist besides. Rumors persisted on the base regarding his dalliances with women and his lackadaisical attitude toward work, but he also maintained a reputation for keeping a cool head and making accurate judgments in the heat of the moment, and as such he had many supporters among his men. Edward knew Roy only as an ambitious climber in the ranks, who was enough of a maverick that he might actually make it to the top one day.

Edward's face remained sour. "So why was I connected

to you, Colonel? I called accounting at the base about my money. You think you could send me back to them?"

"I asked that all calls from you be sent to me. I have a request, actually."

"Absolutely not," Edward responded, without even hearing what the request was. But Roy, having expected this reaction, kept talking over him.

"Where are you now?"

"A bit south of East City. Why?"

"Ah. That's perfect."

He could hear Roy nodding to himself on the other side of the line.

"Perfect for what?"

"Feel like a vacation?"

"Huh?"

"Actually, I need to check something out, but I'm a little tied down here with work. I was hoping I could ask you to go. It's a town in the southeast by the name of Wisteria."

Edward could hear the sound of a pen scratching on paper as Roy spoke. In the background, he heard someone shouting, "Colonel! Did you take a look at that file I gave you yet!?"

"Hang on a second!" he heard the colonel shout back. "I'm looking at it right now! Oh, right," he said to someone else. "Just leave that here, would you?"

Roy put his hand over the receiver and shouted something

that Edward couldn't make out. Then he came back on the phone. "As you can see, I'm up to my neck in it over here," he said to Edward at last.

He seemed even more frantically busy than usual.

"So you need me to help dig you out?" Edward said, grinning.

"Got a shovel?" Roy replied wryly. "You know General Hakuro over at New Optain?"

"Yeah?"

"He's been giving me a lot of trouble lately about how well Southern Command is doing, upping criminal arrests, modernizing, taking on new staff. They're Central's darling these days, it seems. So he's asking why Eastern Command is falling behind, that sort of thing."

"Sounds like they're doing something right at Southern."

"On the outside, sure. But dig a little deeper, and you find that they're just offering rewards to snitches. And with all their modernization, they're finding themselves so understaffed that they've gone to temp agencies on the side to find more people. But the general misses all of that, see? He just hears the good stuff."

Edward sympathized. "Sounds like you've got it rough."

Edward knew a bit about General Hakuro himself: prideful, ambitious, and deadly serious. In comparison to Edward and Roy, he was on the staunch, formal side of things—an old-school military man.

"Isn't Hakuro just doing this to earn himself points with higher command?"

"Without a doubt. But it all adds up to more work for me. That's why I have to monitor this town and put in a report."

"And you want me to do it for you? That's odd for you, Colonel. I'm surprised you're even bothering to do the work in the first place."

Roy never shouldered a task he could slip away from. And Roy knew that Edward knew this, too. He sighed. "Of course I won't do it. It's a pain in the butt. That's why I'm having other people do the work for me, i.e., you. Now, if this town were nearby, I could just send someone out to ask questions and fill in the details here myself, but it doesn't go that easily when it's a place I know nothing about. And I'm afraid the South Area is a bit far. And that's when I remembered that you said you would be going down south. So I thought . . ."

"Ab. So. Lutely. Not." Edward stuck out his tongue at the phone and blew a loud raspberry. "This isn't an official order, right? So, I respectfully decline. Put me on with accounting, please. If your accounting department and this stupid bank here were doing things right, I wouldn't be talking to you now in the first place. In other words, this conversation should never have happened, so give it up."

It infuriated Edward to think that some stupid problem in accounting might have gotten him roped into *this*.

"Actually, that was by my request."

"Huh? What was?" Edward responded, not sure what he meant.

"How else was I supposed to contact you when you're always traveling all over the place? So, I figured I'd better get *you* to call *me*. And what better way to do that than by closing your account?"

Edward's surprise quickly turned to rage. His hand tightened. The receiver made a faint crunching noise in his grip.

"This is . . . This is unacceptable! If I can't get money, Al and I will be forced to slave away at a restaurant because we can't pay our bill!"

"Slave away?"

"Yeah, you heard me!"

Edward told him all that had happened, furious that the colonel would have the gall to cut off his funds, but Roy seemed unperturbed.

"It's a shame you got yourself into that mess, but I think you're getting angry at the wrong person. You really should check your wallet before you sit down to a three-course meal."

Roy was right. Edward glared at the receiver, unable to think of a witty response. The colonel continued. "See, I have a friend over in accounting. Why, if I wanted to, I could ask them to cut off your account forever," he said softly.

Edward knew a threat when he heard one. "So you're

telling me I've got no choice!?"

"Consider it part of your duty as a soldier. You *are* a soldier, aren't you? You should try working for the cause a bit more."

"I don't mind working for the cause. It's *you* I mind working for!"

Roy fell silent. It wasn't that he couldn't think of a retort. He didn't need to speak. This silence made for a more tangible threat than anything he might say.

Edward bit his lip.

Roy took the moment's silence as an opportunity to read off his request. "'The details to be observed include the vagaries of the daily lives of the good populace of the town from the viewpoint of one sharing that . . .' Ahem. My, this is wordy. Basically, you have to go see what's good about the town, what's bad about the town, and how the town leaders made it that way. Oh, and be sure you don't let anyone know that you're with the military! Tell 'em that, and Central will know that it wasn't me who went. Got it?"

"H-hey, wait! That's it!? What about my acc—"

There was a click, and Edward was talking to dead silence. "Colonel . . . you lazy . . . grrah!"

Edward's curse turned into a howl of rage, and he slammed the receiver back down with a crack. The thin tube broke into pieces, sending springs and loops of metal tinkling to the floor. Edward sighed. This was definitely not his day.

TWO DAYS LATER . . .

It still wasn't Edward's day. He paced back and forth atop the hill, muttering under his breath. Perhaps Roy had relented, because when Edward went back to the bank, the teller let him have his money, rescuing him and his brother from forced restaurant labor. However, they had merely traded one onerous task for another. And so they wandered the southern barrens, doing the colonel's bidding, looking for Wisteria.

"Well, it's not like we had our next destination planned out," Alphonse noted. "This could be a good chance for a little vacation. We never get a chance to go somewhere and just stay there."

The brothers had covered a great deal of territory in their quest, but as soon as they had scoured a town for information, they left before they had the chance to enjoy the local scenery or get to know the people. Alphonse seemed to think this was a great chance for them to take it easy awhile, and he pored over the map of Wisteria with eagerness.

"It's supposed to be a small town . . . I wonder what it's like? Maybe it's a bit like Resembool?" Alphonse said, thinking of the brothers' hometown.

"Well, it won't matter what it's like if we never find the place."

Edward squinted his eyes against a sudden, sandy gust of wind. Hesitantly, he opened an eye and looked around. "We've been walking for two days. I can't believe we're not there yet. Where could it be?"

"According to the map, we should be there already. I would think we'd be able to see *something* by now." Alphonse tilted his head, confirming the directions on the map in his hand.

"Well, if we've come this far and we still can't see anything, maybe it's not here anymore?"

With the civil unrest of the last few years finally coming to an end, new towns were springing up all over the place, yet things remained chaotic. People moved from town to town at a moment's notice, and places that were inconveniently situated quickly dropped off the map.

It wasn't hard to imagine something of the sort happening here. No trains ran through this barren expanse of rock and gravel and sand. They had been walking for some time, and yet they had found no signs of civilization.

Edward scanned the horizon. "Hey, Al. Do you know why this place is called Wisteria?"

"Wasn't it something about the town always being in a shadow that gave it this dark purple color—like the Wisteria flower?"

"Right. Know what I think? I think that town couldn't possibly be here. There's nothing in this wasteland to make a shadow big enough to cover a whole town!"

Edward swept his hand around them, indicating their surroundings. The sun shone brightly on the rolling hills. The only shadows came from small boulders sitting atop the sand.

Edward sighed deeply. "They must have abandoned the place. I'm afraid we're going to have to tell the colonel that we can't observe a town that's not there! We better get some sort of bonus for coming all this way. And he better treat us to a meal or two . . ." said Edward, pondering how he would get his due from Roy for sending them on this wild goose chase.

Alphonse interrupted his reverie. "Ed! I see someone!"

"Huh?" Edward squinted against the sun until he could make out the vague silhouette of someone walking toward them. It looked like a traveling merchant. He was carrying a large bundle on his back.

"A merchant . . . out here?"

"The town must be up ahead after all. Let's ask."

"Excuse me!" Edward and Alphonse trotted forward, getting closer to the man. He was walking with his face down to keep the sand from his eyes, but he lifted his head when he heard Edward's and Alphonse's footsteps on the sand.

"Ah? Something the matter?"

"Hello! We want to ask you something . . ."

Alphonse showed the map to the man and pointed at the word Wisteria. "We want to go here, but the thing is, we can't find it . . . Do you know if it's still around?"

"Nonsense!" the man laughed, and tapped the name Wisteria on the map. "It's right here. Just a little bit farther. You don't know about Wisteria?"

"Uh, well, not really."

In fact, the only thing Edward and Alphonse knew about Wisteria was that it was a faraway town to the south . . . a town in a shadow, but of what, they had no idea.

"Well, it's odd for people to come here not knowing anything about the place. You know, she's developed a great deal of late. Whole town's blooming. Some people call it a paradise."

"Paradise?" Edward couldn't help but grin at hearing the word. "In this wasteland?" He swept his arm across the horizon.

The man nodded deeply. "Live there once, and you'll grow so accustomed to easy living, you'll never want to go anywhere else."

"It's that nice a town, huh?"

"And more. From what I hear, no one's left town since the place was founded. Truly a badge of honor in these troubled times. Why, I thought if it was *that* nice, I might do well to make my living there. But, alas, they didn't let me in."

"Wouldn't let you in? Why not?" Edward began to worry. How could they check out the town if they couldn't even get inside?

The man looked back the way he had come with regret in his eyes. "They control who enters the town, you see. They say the policy is that they only let in people in truly dire straits, with no place to go home to. That's why the mayor built the town . . . and so I was told I had no place there. Still, that mayor is a real saint. Not many people these days would even care. Why, I couldn't argue with the man. Still, I did want a chance to get into what some folks've been calling the 'Last Paradise.' I tried asking some townspeople I passed on the road . . . but no good."

"I thought you said no one ever left Wisteria . . ."

"Not for good, no, but there are no phones in Wisteria, so folks have to leave in order to have contact with people outside. It's very rare, but you sometimes see people go by. In fact, I just passed some only a few moments ago. If you hurry, you might catch up to them. Why not ask them if they will let you in?"

"Let's go, Ed!"

"Right!" Edward smiled. Maybe they had a chance of finding—and getting into—the town after all.

The man furrowed his brow, looking a little worried. "I have to warn you, the area outside the town can be a bit dangerous right now. You see, some folks, they've heard about Wisteria's easy life. Think they can sneak into town if they get half a chance. They set up a bunch of tents just outside of town. Harass the townsfolk to no end, they do. Try not to get involved."

Thanking the man for his warning, Edward and Alphonse continued walking, at a slightly quicker pace than before.

"I'm glad the town's really there after all."

"And it's just up ahead!"

"If what that man said was right," Alphonse noted, "we

might have trouble getting inside."

"Well, we have to get in, or we won't be able to do Roy's job for him. Let's try asking those townspeople he told us about."

A short while later, they came to the shantytown: a field of small shacks, tied-up horses, and covered wagons. It looked like the people intended to live here permanently, out in the middle of nowhere.

"You think those are the dangerous people he was talking about?"

"Then Wisteria must be right there . . . but I don't see anything."

Other than the tents, there was nothing: no buildings, no streets, nothing resembling a town.

Edward let out another deep sigh when he heard a sharp voice cry out from up ahead. "Let me through!"

The voice was young, a girl's voice, out of place in this unwelcoming land. A cluster of swarthy men crowded in the direction of the voice. They had the build of men who worked—or stole—with their hands. Their eyes were distrustful and cunning. They clearly were not the good citizens of Wisteria. One held a rifle.

Through the pack of men, Edward caught a glimpse of long hair waving in their midst. *That can't be good*, he thought, observing the evil scowls on the men's faces.

Alphonse stopped beside him, looking at the crowd. "I

wonder what's going on? What's the girl doing here?"

The men formed a ring around the girl, blocking her escape.

"Just let us in, okay? It's not nice to keep all the good stuff to yourselves," they could hear one of them saying.

"You should open the gates while we're still asking nice, see?"

The men were not shouting, but their voices carried an unmistakable threat. However, when the girl responded, her voice didn't sound frightened in the least.

"If you want to go in, then just walk in. We have no fences, no moat. You just can't use *our* way in, that's all." Oddly, from her voice it sounded like the girl was *daring* them.

"But your way is the only way!"

"I'm sorry. I don't know what you're talking about," the girl replied with a toss of her hair.

"Little runt! Just because we *can't* do anything to you don't mean we don't *want* to. You won't be wearing that smile for long."

Edward and Alphonse began walking toward the crowd. They heard the girl continue. She sounded irritated. "You just want to ruin things in our town! Why do you think we should welcome you?"

One of the men shouted back, "I don't like your attitude!" He was poised to lunge at her.

"Uh-oh," Alphonse said. "We have to help that girl!"

Edward frowned. "I don't know. Normally, you don't

THE VALLEY OF WHITE PETALS

talk to people like that when you're surrounded. Maybe she thinks she can take them?"

As they approached the ring of men, Edward clearly saw that the lone girl standing in their midst wasn't scared at all.

"If you want to come in and trade with us, find another way in . . . if you care to risk your lives."

Several of the men clenched their hands into fists.

"Some people you just got to beat the sense into," one grumbled.

"Just cut us in for a piece of the pie, and we'll protect the town from other people! We're offering a service!"

One of the men lifted a fist.

Alphonse rushed forward.

"We don't need your protection," the girl shouted, grabbing the big man by the collar of his shirt as she ducked to the side. The man teetered, off-balance, and she threw him down onto the ground.

"You just want to steal what's ours, without working for yourselves!"

The girl brushed the man's hand off, blocked a rifle butt with her forearm, and lifted her knee into the new assailant's solar plexus. Another man dropped in the dust.

With two of the men down, the circle around the girl began to waver. At last, the brothers could see the girl plainly.

She had long black hair bound in a single ponytail atop

31

her head. Her voice sounded quite young, but now that they saw her, she looked a touch older than they. She was tall for her age, with slender arms and waist, and she stood up straight with an almost noble air. She wore a short-sleeved shirt, and though the rest of her was covered in what looked like military surplus wear, they could see that she was well muscled. More than anything, though, it was her eyes that left the deepest impression on Edward and Alphonse.

Her eyes were as black as her hair, yet they burned with such intensity they seemed almost on fire.

Her long hair swayed right and left as she danced in a circle, knocking down one man after another.

"Don't think we'll let you get away this time!"

"Everyone, help!"

In the space of a few moments, the girl had knocked down several men. Those left standing called to their friends to join them.

"Ed, we should help her!" Alphonse shouted.

Edward did not move. "Help? Help who?"

"What do you mean, 'who'?"

Before their eyes, the girl took down yet another man.

"I don't think she needs helping," Edward observed.

"What if they all jump her at once?" Alphonse asked worriedly.

The girl faced off against a gruff-looking thug when another man snuck up behind her. He hefted a metal pole in his arms, ready to strike her from the back.

Alphonse shouted. "Look out, behind you!"

Alphonse couldn't tell if she had heard him or not. At the last moment, she whirled and lashed out with her foot straight behind her, kicking the man in the shoulder and sending his pole skidding in the dust as he fell flat on his back.

The other men turned to see who had warned her.

"Who's that in the armor?"

"They her friends?"

The man looked suspiciously at Edward and Alphonse.

"Well, not friends, but . . ." Alphonse began, then he shook his head. "You shouldn't all gang up on a girl! It's not fair."

One of the men snorted with laughter. "You stay out of this! Forget them," he said to the others. "Get the girl!"

Now the men looked positively bloodthirsty.

"That's ten against one! You can't do that!" Alphonse shouted.

"Al!" Before Edward could stop him, Alphonse ran right into the middle of the fray.

Edward swore under his breath, but then he smiled. Usually, Edward, with his short temper, got them into these scrapes. This had to be the first time they got into a fight because Alphonse was being *nice*. Shaking his head, Edward ran to join his brother. He might have trouble motivating himself on behalf of the colonel, but this was Alphonse. Besides, two days of aimless wandering had put him in the perfect mood for a fight.

He swung a fist at the first man he reached, sending him reeling. He moved on to the man raising his rifle toward the girl.

"Hey!"

Several people turned to face Edward. They carried long boards and metal poles in their fists.

"Let's beat this punk into the ground!" one shouted.

The men charged. But instead of pulling back, Edward whipped off his coat, threw his right glove on the ground, and broke into a run straight at his assailants. As he ran, he clapped his hands firmly together. There was a sharp noise, and, as the men watched, confused, Edward placed his left hand over his right.

There was a flash of light. When it faded, a sharp blade extended from Edward's right hand. Edward swung.

The man stood bewildered as their poles and boards fell in pieces on the ground.

"An alchemist!" somebody shouted. Edward ran between the confused men. Slashing with his blade-arm, he cut the raised rifle in half and blocked an incoming iron pipe with his right wrist, sending sparks flying.

Edward barreled into the man, knocking him off balance, and swung his left fist up into the man's stomach. The man fell to the ground, wheezing for air.

A fist-sized rock came flying toward him, but Edward ducked smoothly and grinned at the men hiding behind a boulder. "Try again?" he offered, but it looked like they were now more interested in running and hiding than in throwing blunt objects. They had seen how well Edward fought, and they had seen the flash of alchemy, and it had taken the fight out of them.

"Al, now's our chance!"

Edward looked around at Alphonse. His brother nodded and called out to the girl, who had just finished taking down two more men.

"You run too!"

Alphonse started to go back the way they had come, but the girl shook her head. "This way!" she cried, grabbing Alphonse's arm and tugging him in the opposite direction.

"H-hey, wait!"

"Don't talk, just come!"

They ran through the cluster of tents and shacks and ran straight into the barren waste.

"Just a little farther, and they won't be able to follow us."

"Huh? Really?"

Alphonse looked behind to see Edward running after them. Behind him, the men stood watching them run, looks of regret on their faces. Alphonse was relieved they weren't being followed anymore, but at the same time, he was confused. "I don't see where we're running to. Why don't they follow us?"

The only thing in front of them was the same wilderness that they had left.

"Why are we going this way!? Shouldn't we go back the way we came?" Edward shouted angrily as he ran to catch up to them.

But the girl kept running. "Just be quiet and follow me! You ask too many questions."

"Hey, we saved you back there!" Edward shouted furiously, but the girl didn't look back. It was all the brothers could do to keep up with her.

After a short distance, the girl looked around to make sure they were not followed.

"We should be safe now." At last, the girl slowed to a walk. "Thank you for saving me. My name is Ruby."

"I'm Alphonse. And this is . . ." Alphonse shook her hand and motioned to his brother to introduce himself.

Edward scowled. "Listen, you . . ." he said to Ruby. "What were you doing out here? Isn't it a little dangerous to be traveling alone so far from home?"

Running through the wilderness with no idea of where he was going after having just spent two days wandering aimlessly had done little for Edward's mood.

"And furthermore," he added, "that fight back there was partly your fault. How many lives do you think you have, anyway? Keep talking like that and you'll use them all up."

Ruby rolled her eyes. "What are you talking about? They're the ones who are bad. Why should I be nice to them?"

"Well, maybe they are. But to my eyes, coming from the

outside, it was hard to tell who was worse. Actually, now that I think about it, you were definitely the one who started that whole thing."

Alphonse had to stifle a laugh. Edward was the most headstrong, brazen person he knew. They say that, when you meet someone just like yourself, you either get along great or you hate one another. This looked like a case of the latter.

"You're not exactly citizen of the year yourself, Ed."

"Yeah, but I'm nowhere near as cocky as she is."

Ruby frowned. "Who was the one who didn't want to run away from those men?"

"Well, what if I was running with the wrong person! Man, I'm sorry we helped you at all. What a mistake!"

"Sorry you helped? I don't recall asking for your help at all! But Alphonse was nice to come to my aid like that. Thank you, Alphonse."

Edward got madder still. "Hey, I helped you too. You know, for a girl, you're really un-cute."

"Like you'd even know, *little boy!*" Ruby shot back.

The two looked daggers at each other, with Alphonse watching on from the side.

"I'm not a little boy!"

"Really? You're awfully short."

"*Short?!*" Edward's scowl deepened even further at the mention of the word. "You've got a lot of nerve, you know that? You're barely taller than me yourself!"

Edward's hand swung out reflexively to slap her on the shoulder. She blocked the blow mid-swing.

"Ow!"

"Don't think I can't beat you just because I'm a girl!"

The two resumed their staring match.

Alphonse was impressed. He had seen Edward lash out before when people called him "short," and few could block his vengeful swing. But Ruby had brushed it aside like it was a falling twig.

"Can we stop this, please, Ed? Ruby, this is my older brother, Edward."

"Older brother? Are you sure?"

"Yeah, he's sure."

"Really? Because from the looks of it . . ." Ruby looked up at Alphonse, then back at Edward. Edward glared at her.

"Listen, say one more thing about my height, and I'll—"

"I won't. I make it my policy to not tease children."

Alphonse laughed.

"Whatever! We're out of here, Al!" Edward picked up his traveling trunk and started walking off when Alphonse grabbed him gently by the shoulder.

"Where are you going? I thought we came here to find Wisteria."

Alphonse turned to Ruby, his hand still on his brother's shoulder. "You're from Wisteria, aren't you, Ruby?"

The girl turned to look back at Alphonse. "Of course."

"Great! We can rest up here."

"You think that I want to?" Edward snapped.

"Come on, Ed. Ruby can show us the way." He turned to Ruby. "We got kind of lost. We've been looking for two-and-a-half days. Is the town far from here?"

Ruby looked surprised. "Two-and-a-half days? That long?! Why, it's only a day to the nearest town from here, if you go by the short route."

"How could that be?"

"We couldn't see the buildings, so we got a little lost."

Edward and Alphonse sighed together.

"Couldn't see any buildings? You . . . don't know anything about Wisteria, do you?"

"I guess not."

"Then I'll show you. The town is right over there."

"Huh?" Edward and Alphonse scratched their heads in unison, seeing the girl point up a gentle slope.

"Where?"

"I don't see anything."

They stared and stared, but there was nothing in that direction. No town, no people, just a gentle slope up, and a sound, unfamiliar in this dry, dusty place. It sounded just like . . .

"Water? Flowing water, here!?" Edward shook his head. The brothers walked up the slope after Ruby and the sound grew clearer with each step. It was water, all right, though still quite far off.

"We're here." Ruby called from a few steps ahead of them. "Wisteria." She was standing atop a small hill, pointing ahead. Edward and Alphonse climbed up to stand next to her, and gasped at what they saw.

It was a brown, barren waste. Rocks and boulders lay scattered amid yellow dust blown by the wind. It was exactly like the plains behind them, with one exception: there was a giant ravine.

The walls of the ravine were sheer cliffs that seemed to go down forever. Though the sun was still shining on the rise where they stood, the shadow of the rim cast deep shadows over the bottom of the hole.

"Wisteria . . ."

At the bottom of the ravine was a village. From here, they could see that the hole was slightly elliptical. At the bottom, water flowed through the town from one side to the other out of a spot on the cliff wall. A short distance from the wall, a small dam regulated the flow of water, creating a waterway that ran straight through the middle of town before being swallowed into the cliff wall on the far side. Near the dam stood a large mansion. Several other houses had been built down the sides of the waterway. A line of buildings that looked like factories and a large domed furnace stood nearby. There were fields here and there, growing vegetables and fruit, and they could see people with baskets piled high with produce.

A cool wind came blowing up from the bottom of the gorge, bringing with it the sounds of flowing water and workers in the factory.

"Amazing!" Edward couldn't help but gasp.

"Didn't think it was at the bottom of a cliff?"

"No. I can see why it would be dangerous to try to go in," said Alphonse, impressed.

"Now I see what's keeping those bandits out," Edward said.

"There's only one way in." Ruby walked along the edge of the cliff. A short distance ahead of her, two strong-looking men stood. They carried rifles.

"A narrow ridge runs down the cliff wall to the bottom near where they're standing. That's the way down."

"What about the other side?" Edward looked at the far side of the pit. It was too far away to see any detail.

"The far side is even more dangerous. There are too many cracks in the cliff, and holes. That's why we need to guard only one side. Those men back there can't come within range of our rifles."

That was why the invaders had given up their chase. They came closer to the armed guards, until they could see the top of the path. Two stones stood at the entrance, with a pole stretched between them, blocking the way.

"So it's like a natural fortress. But can we go in? I heard there were conditions for getting inside the town."

"That's true, but you saved my life. That satisfies the law—I'm legally bound to thank you."

"The law . . . of the town?"

"Yes." Ruby nodded, smiling brightly, and set off toward the path leading down to Wisteria.

Chapter Two

Paradise Below

EDWARD and Alphonse made their way down the cliff, following Ruby along the narrow ledge. In places where the path became too narrow to walk safely, wooden stairs and pathways gave a tenuous support. By the time they reached the bottom, night had fallen.

The brothers looked up the way they had come and gasped. From above, the town at the bottom of the hole had seemed cramped and narrow. But from down here, the night sky was stunning, a wide ellipse ringed by the black line of the rim. Somehow, the lack of a horizon made it look as though there were nothing holding the sky in place—like it might come crashing down, stars and all.

All Edward could say was "Whoa."

"You're gaping like a fish," Ruby said with a smirk.

Edward snapped his mouth shut. "What was that you said about teasing?"

"Come on, you two," Alphonse said with a laugh. "No more fighting, please."

"What a jerk," Edward grumbled. Inside, he was glad that, for once, he wasn't the troublemaker in the bunch.

Ruby led them into the middle of town. She pointed as she walked. "To the right of where we came out is where the mayor, Mr. Raygen, lives."

A large white mansion stood in the direction Ruby pointed. It towered over the other houses in town, surrounded by a large garden.

"The sluice gate is right behind the mansion," Ruby continued. "That's where they control the flow of the water, to keep the river running through town without washing it away."

Edward stretched his neck to see the large wall of the sluice gate. "What do you with the water that doesn't come through town?"

"There's another waterway that runs under the mansion," she explained. "That's where they send it. The two waterways—the one underground and the one that runs through town—join back together on the far side and leave through the cliff wall," Ruby explained, sweeping her hand from the right side of the village to the left. Edward could just make out a crack where the water flowed into the cliff wall. It seemed that the crack ran all the way from the top of the cliff to the bottom. It was the same on the side of the town where the river began. Edward realized that Wisteria must be part of a longer canyon system. For some reason, the canyon had widened right at this spot, creating the perfect place to build a town.

Edward looked up at the twinkling stars above and got his bearings. He recalled seeing a river on their map. At the time, he'd thought it was odd that they hadn't found any tree line giving away its location during their search for Wisteria. "This river . . . There are some mines further upstream, aren't there?"

"That's right," Ruby said. "Very deep mines, too. We get quite a lot of gravel and sand washing down the river, and sometimes ore and jewels, even. Normally, you'd have to dig pretty deep beneath the earth to find such things, but in Wisteria, they just come floating down the river. It's our most valuable natural resource . . . and the reason why those bandits want to get in so badly."

"So, you collect the gems for sale . . . but how do you get them out?"

Ruby's chest puffed with pride. "That's my job."

"Your job?"

"Once a month, we gather all the ore and gemstones together, and carry them out of town. Of course, the bandits know we're coming. That's why I go along as security. When there is no shipment, I keep things safe down here in the village."

"That's why you're so strong," Alphonse said, impressed.

"Strong-headed," Edward grumbled beside him.

"Ed . . ." Alphonse glared at his brother. "Ruby, aren't you a little young to be a security guard?"

Ruby laughed. "I'm just doing what I can to help Mr. Raygen. He's so nice, you know. He helps people who don't have the means to make it on their own, who don't have a place to go. He gives them work. That's why everyone here is so happy, me included. He helped me when I was still very little, and now I'm repaying the favor. Because of Mr. Raygen, I have a new life. This truly is paradise. Sure, it's a bit inconvenient without electricity, but we get by with alcohol lamps and the like. See?" she said, pointing toward the middle of town. "They're turning on the lights now."

The brothers looked to see a man carrying a long stick with a flame burning on one end. He moved from lamp to lamp, lighting each one as he went. Gradually, the town at the base of the cliffs began to glow with a warm light.

"Paradise in the wasteland," Edward muttered, looking at the town stretched out before him.

They continued walking. Before long, they met their first villagers—some men sitting by the side of the road.

"Hey there, Ruby. Welcome back," said one of the men, noticing them.

"Ruby! They give you any trouble today?" another said with a wave of his hand.

Ruby waved back. "Nothing I couldn't handle! Are you all on break?"

"You bet. We fished up a big rock today, we did. The other

shift is polishing it now," the first man told her.

"It will fetch a pretty price, that one," his friend commented.

"We got some extra time off," said the first, "so I loaded soil for a new field. See?" he said, raising his hands. "When's the last time you saw me with dirty hands?"

"I can't remember the last time I saw you lot *without* dirt all over yourselves," she shot back.

The men laughed, slapping at their grimy clothes. Their faces were dirty, but their eyes had the shine of people who were truly content with their work. The men called out cheerfully to Edward and Alphonse.

"Say, you're a new face!"

"What's that, armor? That's a fine-looking suit!"

"Th-thanks," Alphonse stuttered. He was used to people pointing and staring at him, not complimenting him. The man's eyes went next to his brother's right arm.

"And is that auto-mail? Guess we got something in common, then," he said with a smile, lifting his arms so Edward could see. "I've got some auto-mail m'self. Helps me get those tricky jobs no one else wants, eh? I used to curse the army with every breath for doing this to me, but since I came here, well, it's almost a blessing." He slapped his metal arms together, making a loud ringing noise. "I'm just glad I found a use for these things."

"Yeah," his companion echoed. "Better putting them to good use down here than up there, where a man can work day in and day out and have nothing to show for it."

"I hear that," the first man said, nodding. "And to think it's the law of the town that lets us live like this. Now *that's* a blessing for sure."

"What's this 'law of the town' everyone keeps talking about?" Edward asked their guide. But before Ruby could answer him, one of the men pointed down the road ahead.

"As a matter of fact, Mr. Raygen went down to the town square just now. We had three people come to ask permission to live here. They're probably still there talking."

Ruby's face brightened. "Mr. Raygen? In the square?"

With all the energy of a young girl, she bolted down the road, leaving the brothers behind and Edward's question unanswered.

"So this Raygen guy is the mayor, right?" Edward asked.

"I wonder what kind of fellow he is," Alphonse wondered out loud.

The brothers followed after Ruby until they came out into a large town square.

"Mr. Raygen!" Ruby ran over to a man talking with several others in the middle of the square. "Mr. Raygen, I delivered your letter safely! I brought you a receipt."

"Ah, Ruby! You're back," he said, turning. The one she called Mr. Raygen was an older man, with silver hair down to his shoulders and a face wrinkled by the passing years. He looked around sixty. His blue eyes twinkled as he smiled and reached out a hand from the cloak he wore to keep off the night air, taking the receipt from Ruby. "Thanks, as always. Sorry to send you off on personal business like that." His voice was deep and rough but kind.

"I know you like to keep up correspondence with your old friends, Mr. Raygen. I'm happy to help!" Ruby smiled, pleased with the praise.

"Is that the same girl as before?" Edward muttered to his brother. "She's so sweet all of a sudden."

Alphonse chuckled. Raygen looked up. "I see we have some new visitors."

"Oh, right," Ruby said hurriedly. "I, um, just outside the village, those bandits had me surrounded, and these two came to help. I thought I should thank them . . . Don't worry—they haven't come to live here or anything."

Edward frowned as Raygen gave Ruby a suspicious look. "Maybe we're not going to be able to stay?" he asked quietly, but Raygen shook his head.

"No, no, you're welcome, of course. Normally, we like to screen visitors to the village, but Ruby says you helped her out of quite a scrape. To turn you back now would go against the law of the town. Stay with us awhile. You must be tired from your journey here."

"Sorry . . . the 'law of the town?'" Edward said, still curious about this law that everyone in the village felt was so important.

"Ah, yes," Raygen replied softly. "Here in Wisteria, we base all our interactions on the principle of equivalent exchange."

"Equivalent exchange?" Edward and Alphonse said together, startled to hear such a familiar term used so out of context.

All alchemy works on the principles of conservation of matter, so the concept of equivalent exchange was central to much of the work alchemists performed.

"I'm a little confused," Alphonse said honestly. "How does equivalent exchange apply to a civil law? That's the first time I've ever heard it used that way."

Raygen's warm smile faded, and a slightly sad look crept into his eyes. He turned and looked over the square. "Yes, it is uncommon, as you say. Yet as surely as one equals one, there is an equivalent for all things in our world down here. Not so in the world above, however. In exchange for peace, the military kills. In exchange for hard labor to build industry, workers are underpaid. The world overflows with absurdities."

Raygen fell silent. "Some despair, thinking that the absurdities of the world are their fault because they lacked the strength to do what others told them to do. My experience with alchemy taught me the wonders of equivalent exchange, and so now, I pass on what I've learned to improve the welfare of all our people, to give them hope."

"You know some alchemy, don't you, Edward? Don't you

THE VALLEY OF WHITE PETALS

know about equivalent exchange?" Ruby said, giving Edward a playful slap on the shoulder. She must have seen him using alchemy in the fight with the bandits above.

Raygen's eyes opened wide. "An alchemist? You?"

"Uh, yeah, sort of . . ." Edward mumbled. Clearly, the folks living here in Wisteria had little love for the military. If they found out that he was a State Alchemist, Ed and Al would lose their welcome here for sure. They would probably wonder exactly why a State Alchemist was coming here in the first place, and then the jig would be up. Central would find out that Roy hadn't gone to check out the town himself, and there would be hell to pay . . . out of Edward's pocket, no less.

Raygen took the look of consternation on Edward's face as a sign that he had only dabbled in alchemy and didn't understand the finer points of the science. After all, he was only a boy to Raygen's eyes.

"Perhaps you know a little about it, yes?" Raygen asked, smiling.

"Just a little," Edward mumbled. He glanced up at Alphonse and signaled with his eyes to keep quiet. He didn't want to start out on the wrong foot with the people in this town.

"During my studies of alchemy," Raygen began, sounding for the world like a teacher talking to a slow student, "I realized that the law of equivalent exchange provided a perfect, easily understandable set of guidelines under which a community of people could live together in harmony. With equivalent exchange, I could create an even, fair society where each received his due for his work and efforts. I wanted to help the people I saw struggling with the unfairness of the world above. As a novice alchemist yourself, try applying what you know of the law of equivalent exchange to what you see around you in this town. Ahem."

Raygen straightened and turned to the three men with whom he had been speaking before Edward and Alphonse arrived. "As I was saying, our town was founded to help those unable to help themselves. Only those in true need are allowed to enter. You understand, I trust?"

The three looked at each other—these must be the applicants for residency, thought Edward. One of the men was so thin he seemed as though he might collapse at any moment. Another appeared to be a merchant, wheeling a broken-down cart piled with goods behind him. The third appeared to be a traveler of some sort, carrying a walking stick and little else.

The merchant scowled and spoke. "So, you mean to tell me that a merchant like myself isn't welcome?"

"I'm sorry," Raygen replied. "But if you have a home to go back to, we have nothing for you here. As you can see, our available space is quite limited. And why have you come to our town?" he asked, turning to the traveler.

"I heard Wisteria was a paradise," the traveler replied,

taking off his hood as he spoke, "I thought I might be able to make some cash."

"You have family?"

"A wife, sir . . ."

"Then go back to her. A man should live in his own home, am I wrong?"

"Y-yeah, but . . ." the man stuttered.

"You do not require what Wisteria has to offer," Raygen said gently. "Your wife can provide you with all that you truly need."

He turned to the last man. "And you?"

"I'm without home or family . . . Lost both in the war, and what's the military give me? Nothing. I figured something was wrong with the world . . . and that's when I heard about this town," the man said, between nervous looks at Raygen's face.

Raygen answered him with a warm smile. "You have no home? Then you may live with us. There is much work for you to do here."

"Yeah . . . work. Er . . ." the man stuttered sheepishly.

"Something the matter?"

He grimaced and scratched at his neck furiously. "There's something I should tell you," he said at last. "I, uh, at the last place I worked, someone took my job, and I, uh, I got mad and . . ."

Raygen held out his hand to silence him. "You have no

place to go home to. That is reason enough for you to join us."

"Wait a second!" the merchant butted in. "This man could be a criminal! You'd let criminals walk right in, but you keep a respectable citizen like myself out? I traveled a long way here just to earn a little bread. Look at my cart: it's half ruined!" The man spat, his face red with anger. "Everyone knows how well off you Wisteria folks are. If you don't open up your gates soon, those bandits will break them down for you! You say you want to help people? Feh!"

"Was that a threat!?" Ruby shouted, glaring suspiciously at the merchant. "Who are you to talk to us like that, anyway? The problem is with the world outside, not with us in here. They talk about peace, sure, but then the military comes in and wrecks everyone's lives! Mr. Raygen only wants to help the victims, can't you see that? I'll never forget what he's done for me—and if bandits want to come and take our paradise away, let 'em come! I'll fight them off myself!"

"That's enough, Ruby," Raygen said, putting his hand on Ruby's shoulder.

"But Mr. Raygen!"

"I appreciate your spirit, Ruby. Though I do pity the man you choose to spend your life with," he said with a chuckle.

"Why, why would I spend any time with anyone but you, Mr. Raygen? I owe you so much."

"That's not what I was talking about," Raygen said, not unkindly. "You're a very pretty girl, Ruby. Pretty like a rose, but those thorns of yours are likely to scare off potential partners. And I look forward to seeing you start a happy family here in Wisteria. I know you had it hard outside."

Raygen paused, then reached a hand out and touched the merchant's broken cart, piled high with goods. Edward and Alphonse noticed an alchemical circle drawn on the sleeve of his cloak.

"You traveled far to come here. Few people know what it is we truly do here at Wisteria. They merely come, lured by tales of wealth and riches. I understand why you're upset. Allow me to fix your cart for you."

There was a brief flash of light on the cart.

The man yelped. When Raygen took his hand off the cart, the broken wheel looked as good as new.

"Again, we welcome within our borders only those who cannot find happiness outside. Please understand."

Raygen called the guards at the entrance of the square to show the two men he had refused out of town. He handed the third man over to the care of another guard before turning back to Edward and his brother.

"I'm sorry to take your time. Please, enjoy Wisteria during your stay. We are grateful for your help. You need not worry about food or money while you stay with us."

So saying, Raygen turned and with slow steps made his way back to the large mansion at the head of the river.

EDWARD AND ALPHONSE were taken to a small home near the waterway, a short distance downstream from the town center. It appeared that someone had been living here before—there were shelves and beds and a lamp already waiting for them.

"There's a restaurant to the right of the square," Ruby told them as she lit the lamp. "And there's a bucket outside. Just go to the waterway if you need any water." She turned back around. "Well? What did you think of Mr. Raygen?" she asked, pride resonating in her voice.

"He's awfully kind to take in people like that," Alphonse said.

"Yeah," Edward agreed. "It's not easy to find homes for all the homeless people these days." Edward *was* impressed. He couldn't condone turning a blind eye to someone with a possible criminal record, but the man's generosity was overwhelming.

Ruby smiled. "Isn't he great? Truly a remarkable man! He's actually accomplishing what no one in the world above can hope to do—he's created a society of equals here. Up there, there's all this theft and bribery and corruption. In the end, it's the people at the bottom who pay. They lose their jobs, their families, their homes. But here, we have a clear rule to guide us: equivalent exchange. That's why we all work hard, even on the really tough jobs, because we know we'll be rewarded in kind. It's amazing that with all those people and all that money, the military couldn't do what Mr.

Raygen is doing all by himself here."

"You really respect him, don't you?" Alphonse said cheerfully.

"I do. That's why I swore never to leave his side. And . . ."

Ruby grew suddenly quiet. She looked down at the floor and fidgeted for a moment before looking up at Alphonse and then Edward.

"What?" asked Edward with a scowl. He was ready for another bout of name calling, and so what she did say took him by surprise.

"Thank you . . ." she said at last with some difficulty. "Thank you for helping me. I swore to stand by Mr. Raygen forever. And to think, if those bandits had stopped me there, I might never have been able to see him again," she explained, a look of determination in her eyes. "I know I was kind of mean back there, but I really am grateful."

"No, no, it's okay," Alphonse said, waving his hands. "We just happened along at the right time. We're the ones who should thank you for showing us into town. See, we help each other out." He looked down at his brother. "Right, Ed?"

"Right," Edward said. "I liked it better when you were being a jerk, anyway. You made me look good."

"Whaddya mean, a jerk?!" Ruby shouted, raising a fist.

Edward quickly shuffled back, out of range. "Hey, I thought you were grateful!"

"That was before you called me a jerk!"

"Hey, I meant well," Edward insisted.

"If that's the kind of thing you say when you mean well, I never want to hear you when you don't!"

Alphonse stepped in. "Now, now. Say, Ruby, what are you up to now?"

"I should go soon—it's almost time for my shift on guard patrol. I should say my farewells." Ruby pointed up at the rim of the high cliffs. They could barely make out the shape of the security guards at the top, carrying their rifles as they paced to and fro along the line where the deep blue of the nighttime sky joined the black wall of the cliff. Occasionally, they would stop and brandish their weapons, as though scaring off would-be interlopers.

"I'll be off now," she said.

"Yeah, thanks for the room!" Alphonse said, waving.

Ruby smiled. "Bye now, Alphonse." Edward couldn't help but notice the way she stressed Alphonse's name and didn't mention him, Edward, at all.

"Ed, please . . ." Alphonse muttered, chuckling to himself as he went back inside. "I'm just glad that we have a place to stay. So what are you going to do? Do we begin observing? Or can we take a break?"

"Well, you know the colonel. I think we should start observing straightaway. How about we begin at the restaurant?" Edward said with a grin. Just then, his stomach grumbled loudly. The two laughed and set down their luggage, before heading toward the restaurant near the town square.

THE RESTAURANT was quite large and filled with a lively crowd of workers seated at tables piled high with food.

"Evening, gentlemen," a woman in her mid-forties sitting near the entrance called out to them as they entered. "Mr. Raygen told me you'd be coming. He told us about you helping Ruby out, too. Dinner's on the house! What would you like?" The woman smiled warmly and handed them a menu.

"Oh, we're happy to pay for our food," Edward said, hesitating. Visions of the head chef at that restaurant accusing them of being deadbeat diners flashed through his head.

The woman thrust the menu into his hands. "We go by the law of equivalent exchange in this town. You helped out one of the townspeople, so now we'll help you."

Edward nodded and accepted the menu. He *was* famished. "Then, I'll take this vegetable soup and the oven-baked lamb, and could I have some potatoes and a cup of coffee with that?"

"Sure thing!" she replied, writing down Edward's order and turning to Alphonse. "And you?"

"Oh, I'm not hungry."

"You sure? Okay. Well, just let me know if you change your mind."

The woman left, and Alphonse turned to his brother. "Just the lamb? You sure that's going to be enough, Ed?"

"Yeah, it's fine," he said, standing on his tiptoes to whisper in his brother's ear. "See, I was kind of afraid they might ask us to pay later on. So I only ordered as much as I could afford with the money in the wallet."

"Aha, I see," Alphonse said, chuckling. "I haven't seen any banks in town, for that matter."

"Exactly. That means, if it comes to it, we really might have to eat and run—and that would be kind of hard when the whole town is surrounded by cliffs."

"I can tell you're still traumatized by that restaurant," Alphonse said laughing.

Edward scowled. "Yeah, and I know just who I have to blame for it, too."

The two brothers laughed. The woman came back with potatoes and vegetable soup. Edward picked up his fork and prepared to dig in when he was interrupted by a man at the next table.

"Ah, I see you're eating one of my potatoes!" He was grinning and holding a glass of wine in one hand. "We don't get a lot of sunlight, but still I think they turned out pretty nice. How they taste?"

"Mmph, sweet!" Edward said through a full mouth of potatoes.

The man laughed. "Aren't they? Got to eat good if you want to do good work! You'd better eat your fill, too, there," the man added, leaning over to give Alphonse a clap on the shoulder. By now, a few other people had turned to look at the new visitors.

"That's right," said one. "We're all working to help Mr. Raygen's dream come true."

"Can't work on an empty stomach, and can't earn a livelihood if we don't work. If we don't earn a livelihood, this town is through."

"See? Right there is the top-earning man in Wisteria, and look how much he's eating!"

One of the men pointed toward a large fellow eating a whole chicken. He looked sturdy, with a square-cut jaw and ropy muscles on his arms—by all accounts, a man built for doing hard labor.

"Hey, Neil!" someone shouted.

"Huh?" The man washed down a mouthful of chicken with his wine and turned to look over at Edward and Alphonse. "Hey, those the guys that saved Ruby? Ruby told me all about it. She says you two are all right."

Neil walked over, carrying his glass of wine, and pulled a chair up to Edward and Alphonse's table.

"All right, huh?" Edward said, wincing, remembering how she had chewed him out before they came into town.

Neil saw the look on his face and laughed out loud. "Hah! She's a tough one, that Ruby, and I don't just mean her fighting. But the girl's dedicated to Mr. Raygen. She's one of the best security people we've got."

"Yes, we talked to her about Mr. Raygen. She really admires the man."

"Yeah, something about Mr. Raygen saving her a long while back," Neil explained, nodding. "Of course, pretty much all of us here can say the same."

Neil leaned over and rolled up the cuffs of his trousers. Both legs were gleaming auto-mail. "My legs got shot off by stray gunfire during the war. Lost my family, too, every last one. But the army wouldn't do a thing for me. Sent me a letter telling me they'd done what they must to put down unrest, and they were sorry for my loss—that's all! I got real depressed then, started hating everything, and that's when Mr. Raygen offered me a job. Was I grateful? You bet! Still am, too. I know that the more work I do, the more I'll earn here. It's simple, but it works, and *I* work. Now I'm glad I have strong legs that never get tired from too much work."

Another man to the side spoke. "I've still got all my arms and legs in the right places, but my family, they got real sick. I tried to buy the right medicine for them, but I just couldn't make enough money—no matter how hard I worked—to make ends meet and pay for the treatments. In the end, my family died. I blamed myself, 'course. I got in a bad way, then, doing whatever it took to survive. But I knew what I was doing was wrong, and so I came here, to Wisteria— my last hope. And Raygen, he took me in. I'll never get my family back, but now I know it wasn't my fault I couldn't provide for them. It's that twisted world up there. And now I've got something else to work for: making this town the best place it can be."

The man smiled through his entire sad tale. The people listening nearby nodded as he spoke. *They must all have similar experiences,* thought Edward. And they all must thank Mr. Raygen from the bottom of their hearts.

"He's a saint, Mr. Raygen. Helping people who can't help themselves."

"You bet."

Edward looked up and saw that the woman who had taken his order had brought his lamb. She put the plate on the table. "And Mr. Raygen helps too. He says that alchemy should be for the people, so he fixes our houses and our tools for us."

"Impressive," Edward said, and he meant it. Few people who practiced proper alchemy in this day and age took the time to help the public like that. He liked, also, to hear people talking about alchemy in such a favorable light. Too often, he and Alphonse heard stories about alchemy being used for the wrong reasons by the wrong people.

"This really is a great town. I envy you all," Alphonse said. Neil smiled and slapped him on the shoulder.

"So, what's your name, anyway?"

"Oh, I'm Alphonse."

"Alphonse! I've seen you walking around in that armor

like it was no more than regular clothes—you must be pretty strong. Why, you could make a fine living in Wisteria with a body like that. How about it? Why not join us and live here?"

He must think we're like them, Edward thought, *victims of the war.*

"Wisteria opens its doors to people without a home, to people who have seen the injustices of the world above, and looking at you two, I'd say you've seen your fair share," Neal said, confirming Edward's suspicions. "You might have come here by chance, but I think if you tried, you might find it's the right fit."

"Y-yeah, maybe," Alphonse muttered, nodding. No one looking at them would guess the real reason for their auto-mail bodies: they had broken the taboo of human alchemy. Alphonse wasn't about to tell these men that.

"Of course you would." Neil grinned. "With a body like that, you'd make top earner in no time. You earn what you make here, don't forget. Equivalent exchange!"

"But if I were the top earner, wouldn't that mean that I would be making more than you, Neil?" Alphonse asked, sounding worried. "I wouldn't want to have to compete."

The men around them laughed, and Neil shook his head, smiling. "Fine by me. It's all for the good of the town, and Mr. Raygen. And after all, we all live a newer, better life here. How could I have hard feelings?" Neil stood. "So, I propose a toast! To our new prospective citizens, Alphonse, and . . . "

"Edward," Edward said through a mouthful of lamb.

"Yes, Edward! Though you look a bit *slight* for any real hard work . . ."

"Whoa! Whoa!" Alphonse shouted, waving his arms. The last thing he needed was Edward blowing his top in the middle of their welcoming toast. He looked at his brother, but Edward was so engrossed in his lamb that he hadn't heard the comment.

Edward looked up. "Something wrong, Al?"

"Oh, uh, nothing," Alphonse said, visibly relieved.

Neil raised his glass. "Here's to our new guests!"

"To Wisteria and Mr. Raygen!"

"To a good day's work!"

"To the future!"

The men around them joined in, giving toast after toast, their joyful faces showing no trace of the sadness they had known in their former lives.

"I'M STARTING TO THINK that maybe this town is really as great a place as it seems, Ed," Alphonse told his brother as they walked back to the house that served as their lodgings. Edward smiled. The cool night air felt good after the warmth of the restaurant.

Alphonse stopped on the small bridge spanning the waterway that crossed the middle of the town square and looked back the way they had come. Even though it was already the middle of the night, there were still people in the restaurant. The sound of laughter spilled into the square, echoing off the cobblestones.

"The woman who served us said that most of the people here are men who've lost their families . . . That's why everyone eats so late. They don't have anyone to go home to."

Alphonse turned his gaze away from the restaurant and looked up at the night sky. "These people can carry so much pain inside, yet still they manage to greet every morning with a smile. They seem to live healthy, productive lives . . . It's really amazing."

The stars shone brilliant in the night sky, glimmering jewels on a carpet of deep blue. In the town below, fires still burned in the furnaces. Their light spilled out of the factory doors each time the doors opened and spread into the night, along with the sound of the fires crackling.

Neil and several others had left the restaurant when they did. They had said they intended to polish the gemstones they had found that day. They were probably working in the furnaces, Edward assumed.

"Everybody works so hard here," Alphonse said, looking up at the lights around the mansion and factories near the head of the waterway. Suddenly, he slapped Edward on the shoulder. "Ed, look!"

"Huh?"

Edward had been looking in the opposite direction, toward the quiet part of town downriver. He turned around to see Alphonse pointing at one of the factories. As they watched, the upper part of the factory's domed roof slowly rose. Moments later, a tremendous plume of steam came billowing out, and a sharp, cracking noise shot across the town.

"Heat plus water makes steam—they must be using it to process the stones there," Alphonse reasoned.

"Yeah," Edward said, nodding. "It looks like a first-rate operation they've got going there. They must get some nice gemstones coming down the river."

By their nature, ore veins running through the ground rarely came to the surface. If you wanted the precious metals and gemstones they held, you had to dig them out by hand—but the deeper veins were difficult to reach. Here in Wisteria, the river did all the digging for them, delivering the deepest ores and gemstones right into their hands.

"Still, it's not easy work moving rock and gravel that's been soaked in water for any length of time. Equivalent exchange or no, those people in there are working hard for what they earn, I bet."

Several nice houses stood around the mansion near the head of the waterway. That's where the top earners must live, Edward thought.

"Since Mr. Raygen has guards who carry all the town's produce out for him, everybody here working the gemstones depends on him, don't they . . ."

Edward turned toward the main road, thinking about how

the town's economy worked as he walked, mumbling softly to himself. Alphonse turned back to him and laughed.

Edward looked up and frowned. "What?"

"That look in your eyes is the same one you get when you're working on an alchemical problem. I'm starting to think this observation job is perfect for you. And that hand on your chin—just like the colonel!"

Edward started, quickly pulling his hand off his chin and shaking it in disgust. "Give me a break!" he said, scowling.

Just then, he heard a small voice call out, "Ruby." They had just stepped out onto the main road leading up to Raygen's mansion at one end and the town homes where Edward and Alphonse were staying at the other. Alphonse was far enough ahead of Edward that he hadn't heard the voice, so only Edward stopped to look.

He turned around to see the front of a large house protected by a large iron gate. A small boy stood before the gate, dwarfed by the high metal rails.

In the light of the street lamps, the boy's hair shone a brownish gold. He was about Edward's height, but from the size of his hands and his face Edward guessed he was younger—around 12 or 13 years old. His wavy hair curled up at the bottom, blowing gently in the wind.

Ruby stood in front of him, her hand on the half-opened gate, looking down at the boy. She wore a slight, irritated frown. She didn't notice Edward standing on the road.

As Edward watched, the boy reached out both hands to

Ruby. He held a bouquet of flowers.

"Here."

Ruby sighed. "How many times do I have to tell you? Making bouquets doesn't do any good for the town. You need to find some other work to do."

Her voice was different from when she talked to Alphonse or the other townsfolk. It was cool and flat.

"But this is the only work I can do," the boy said in a voice so quiet it was hard to hear. He held out the flowers again, insistently.

"What am I to do with you?" Ruby said, fishing a coin out of her pocket and handing it to the boy. "Here. Now find a job that helps Mr. Raygen, please."

The boy handed the small bouquet of flowers to Ruby. Ruby accepted them, then she did something odd. She pulled out only the white flowers, and gave them back to the boy.

"I don't need the white ones. I don't like them. Later."

Ruby closed the iron gate with a clang and, holding the bouquet dangling loosely from one hand, went back inside the house.

The boy stood a moment looking at the coin in his hand, then walked down the road toward the town square, shuffling his feet in the dirt, his eyes cast down at the road.

"Ed, what is it?" Alphonse called, finally noticing that Edward had stopped.

"Nothing . . ." Edward said, shaking his head. He couldn't

put his finger on it, but something about the scene at the gate left him unsettled. He started walking again, looking back at the gate over his shoulder.

The gate and the fence around it stood nearly two meters high, shutting out the rest of the town. They rattled faintly as the wind blew through the bars.

THE FOLLOWING MORNING found Edward sitting on the bed in their house. Alphonse had left earlier, saying he would begin their work by going to see Neil's workplace. Edward had slept poorly after their late night, so he merely groaned and watched Alphonse leave from under his covers.

He was wide awake, now, the sun already high in the sky, but he still hadn't left the house. He hadn't told his brother about the nasty blister on his right foot. They had been wandering around the mounds for days before getting this assignment, and the two extra days of trudging through the wasteland to find Wisteria hadn't helped matters.

I wonder if my shoes don't fit anymore, thought Edward, sticking his foot in a bucket of water to cool it and grinning a little. Secretly, he fantasized that he would grow so fast he would have to buy new shoes twice a year just to keep up with his feet. "Oops, there goes another pair. I keep buying them and buying them, but I just can't keep up!" he would say to the clerk at the shoe store, and they'd share a knowing laugh.

Thinking that the blister on his foot was a sign of growth

made it easier to bear. Edward smiled and pulled a writing pad and pen out of his traveling trunk. He then placed the trunk on the bed, using it as a makeshift desk.

"Time to write my Wisteria observation report," he said to himself. If he was going to be stuck here until he finished this miserable chore, he might as well get it over with as quick as possible.

"Let's see, the good parts and the bad parts . . . and something about the town leaders. I should probably complain about the colonel, too. This *is* my chance . . .

"Let's see, the good parts first. Mr. Raygen has a good idea with this 'equivalent exchange' concept of his, and the town really seems to be pulling it off. And there's the fact that the town takes in people who have had it rough in the world outside, people who don't have a place to go home to—that's got to be good. Everyone works happily in Wisteria, and they're all paid their fair due . . ."

Edward stopped suddenly and looked at what he'd written. "Funny," he muttered. "Looking at this, it seems almost too good to be true."

From what he was writing, this place really did look like paradise on earth, but for the first time, Edward realized that he wasn't buying it. He shook his head. "Maybe I'm being too cynical . . ."

He put down the pen, flopped down on the bed, and thought back to what Alphonse had said before he left the house that morning.

"You know, Ed," he had joked, "if we stayed here long enough, even I might smile." Indeed, Neil and the other men they had eaten with the night before all seemed as happy as could be to live in this town and work for Mr. Raygen. Alphonse had been deeply impressed. When he left that morning to watch Neil at work, Edward knew Alphonse was only half going to observe for the colonel. Alphonse must have been curious himself to know more about life in Wisteria.

"Maybe it *is* as good a town as Al says it is . . ."

Edward stretched his arms and looked out the window. From his room, he could see the top of the sheer cliff wall, and above it, a clear blue sky.

Edward understood why Alphonse liked this town so much. In the world above, homeless men lingered on every street corner, ripped from their lives by the war and poverty. He didn't mean to ignore them, but it never seemed as though he could realistically do much to help these people. When his kindhearted brother saw those destitute and broken men, he saw people who hurt inside even more than he did. That's why, to him, this town must seem like heaven.

Raygen helped the people that everyone in the world outside ignored. He took them into his town and gave them work. Once the people he saved realized that they would receive fair pay for the work they did, even if the work was hard, it gave them hope. They forgot their pasts and simply lived each day to the fullest.

Edward lay on his side on the bed, watching a cloud slowly drift across the sky. The cloud reached the edge of the cliff and slid out of sight. Edward's eyes went down to the cliff side. Now that it was daytime, he could clearly see the little ridges and irregularities he couldn't see before. The sun reflected hot off the rocks, but here and there, patches of darkness pooled where small shelves of rock cast shadows.

Edward sat there dreamily gazing up, when something small and white entered his field of vision.

Edward sat up, took his foot out of the bucket, and opened the window. Another white thing flew down and came right in through the window, landing next to him on the bed.

"What's this?"

Edward reached to pick up the tiny object when another followed it through the window, drifting down to land on the floor.

"Snow?"

Edward looked up at the sky, but all the clouds were small and fluffy. There was not a storm cloud in sight, and besides, it was still far too warm for it to be snowing.

He picked the object up and brought it close to his face. It smelled sweet.

"A . . . flower?"

He realized that what he held in his hand was a tiny white flower petal. Edward stood and stuck his face out the window, wondering where it could have blown in from, when he saw a boy standing at the foot of the cliffs downstream.

"It's him!" Edward said, remembering the boy from last night who had given the bouquet to Ruby.

ALPHONSE stood in the sorting room of one of the factories near the mansion. Here, they separated gemstones from the gravel taken from the river. He had been helping the workers carry rocks since he'd arrived that morning.

"I've got a good one here!" he called out.

"Great, put it on that table over there," one of the men directed.

"Sure thing!"

Alphonse carried the lump of wet rock to a nearby table. There, several dozen men and women worked at separating the rocks. It was hard work. Even though a cool breeze blew in through the open windows, everyone there had worked up a good sweat.

"This is tough," Alphonse said to the woman who had served him the night before in the restaurant. She worked here in the sorting room, too, it seemed.

"Nah," she said, her hands still moving, sorting the stones. "We got it easy out here. It's much worse farther in."

Alphonse found that hard to believe. The sorters had to pick up heavy piles of rock—some larger than their own heads—and inspect each one carefully, sometimes cracking them open with a pick to see if they held gemstones. Then they sorted all of the rock shards into the appropriately labeled containers.

"Why do you work here?" Alphonse asked, innocently. "Can't you earn a living just by working at the restaurant?"

The woman smiled. "Oh, I could. This work helps the town directly, so it pays the best, to be sure. Still, the people who grow food and work in restaurants all support the workers here, so they get their fair share, too. I'm just helping out to make Mr. Raygen's dream come true a little faster."

She pointed to a box filled with sorted rocks. "You think you could carry those to the next dome over for me?"

"Sure thing." Alphonse put the tray of stones on a metal cart and pushed it out of the factory. Stepping outside, he could hear the sound of water crashing against the sluice gate nearby. The gate was large enough to handle all the water that came out of the underground stream here, but still, standing this close, the force of the water against the gate would impress anyone.

When the water first came into the valley, it was filled with gravel, ore, and rocks of all shapes and sizes. Sodden with water, most of the rocks fell out of the upper stream just before the sluice gate, going down to pass under the factories with the underground river that crossed the town. The rocks then fell into grooves carefully carved into the bottom of the waterway. From there, they rolled into boxes set out to catch them. Men would then haul the boxes out of the water, carry them into the factories, and dump them onto the sorting tables.

In the factories, men and women used magnifying

glasses and sunlight coming through the skylights to sort the piles into ore-bearing rocks and gemstones, sending on the valuable ones to be polished up in preparation for being sold.

Alphonse pushed his cart into the next factory. He could tell from the wavering air that it was very hot inside the dome. Along one side of the factory stood several burning furnaces, each one set to a different temperature. Here was where the actual refining of ores occurred. The heat created here generated steam to polish the gemstones. The trip down the river filled the rocks with a considerable amount of water, and getting the steam out of them and out of the factory took a group effort. Every few hours, everyone in the dome would come together and crank a large wheel that opened the roof. Just seeing how hard they had to tug to move the gears that opened the roof made Alphonse feel tired.

"Neil! Brought some more rock for you," Alphonse shouted from the dome entrance. Neil, hammer in hand and sweating from the effort of shattering stones, had stopped to check on one of the furnaces. The roar of the furnace all but drowned out the sounds of steel on stone.

"'Lo there! Thanks a bunch! Bring it over here, would you?" Neil beckoned Alphonse over, setting down his hammer. Alphonse pushed his cart over.

"See? You're perfect for this kind of work. Only a few of us here can handle one of these beasts." Neil grinned, seeing how easy it was to push the cart with Alphonse helping.

"You always load this many stones in a cart?"

"Aye. I go from here to the sluice gate fifty times every day."

"Fifty times!? Wow. Take care not to hurt yourself."

Alphonse had made the trip only a few times himself, but he could well understand what a difficult task that would be. Pushing these carts demanded not only strength, but considerable skill. The carts wobbled, and if you lost your balance, the rocks might spill. That was fine if your hands and feet were made of auto-mail, but if one of those rocks landed on a foot made of flesh and bone, it would mean a trip to the hospital for sure.

Neil looked startled for a moment, and then he began to laugh. "It's been a while since anyone worried about me. My wife used to tell me to watch out all the time."

"Oh, I'm sorry, I didn't mean to remind you . . ."

Neil shook his head. "Not at all, not at all." They finally arrived with their load before the furnaces. Neil paused to wipe the sweat off his forehead with a towel. "That's all in the past now. Oh, the time I wasted, chasing after my legs and the family I lost. That was before I realized I had to understand who I am now, accept it, and think about moving on."

"Moving on . . ." Alphonse repeated.

"Aye."

Neil looked at the men working in front of the other furnaces, and dabbed at his forehead with the towel. "I thank Mr. Raygen for helping me realize that. The others here are all the same," he said, pointing to two men standing at another furnace. "Some of them, the military had targeted as dissidents, taken them away from their families. They lived rough lives . . . but not anymore. Trying to get back the past will get you nowhere."

One man sat, cutting a gem out of the large boulder and talking to the man next to him, who laughed a loud and carefree laugh. Neil looked at Alphonse. "We're making a new world here, Alphonse. Won't you join us? Help make Mr. Raygen's dream a reality."

"Making a new world . . . ?"

"The world above—the world the military made—all it's got is disorder and confusion. Mr. Raygen sees a world without trouble, without chaos. One where no one has to lose a family or rely on the laws of an oppressive government. We can live by the law of equivalent exchange. It's simple, yeah, but it's strong. In Mr. Raygen's world, everyone can grab a bit of happiness for themselves with their own two hands."

"My own two hands," Alphonse repeated. "I'd never really thought of grabbing anything like that with . . . these," he said, flexing his armored fingers.

"But you can!" Neil took the towel from around his neck and wiped the grime off Alphonse's armored gloves. "I don't know why you wear that suit of armor. I don't know what's in your past, and I don't care to know, either. In Wisteria, you are who you are *now*, here, today. Nobody wants to go back to the past. Why would we? We think about the work we can do now. *That's* living, and we know how good that is."

Alphonse recalled now that, the night before, they were practically exchanging toasts with the other men at the restaurant before anyone even bothered to ask them their names. And when they met Ruby outside the town, they had exchanged names, but she hadn't asked them anything else. Normally, when they met someone, they would have to field a mountain of questions about Edward's auto-mail or Alphonse's armor, but Ruby never showed the slightest interest in either. Was it because the people in this town didn't look to the past? Because they only looked forward?

Neil turned and looked at Alphonse. "Have you accepted who you are?"

Alphonse fell silent. He couldn't say he had. His eyes went down to the floor. Under the domed roof, the floor was bare earth, covered with a layer of gravel made by the leavings from countless stones that had been shattered to reveal the gems and ores inside.

Alphonse looked at his feet, standing on the gravel. The trips by the sluice gate had covered his legs and feet with a spray of water droplets that had been catching dust from the air as he walked. Yet he hadn't noticed the icy water or the layer of grime coating his feet until he looked down . . . because his armor lacked the sense of touch.

He felt nothing. He was never hungry. He never slept. He couldn't even tell whether something in his hand was hot or cold. How could he just accept this? His body shone bright in the light that spilled from the furnaces, yet he was dull to the world. That was why he and Edward had traveled so far in search of a way to get back what they once had been.

ALPHONSE helped Neil with his work a bit longer, then walked back to the house, thinking. The usual sounds filled the town: clanging and the roar of fires from the factory, water rushing down the waterway, and the far-off howling of the wind as it blew down the sheer cliffs. But the streets themselves were quiet. Everyone had work to do. They tilled the fields or sorted and hammered in the factories. Reaching the empty town square, Alphonse found a bench and sat down, looking at his hands in silence. He wasn't sure how much time had passed when a high, clear voice rang out in the square, calling to him.

"Alphonse!"

Ruby ran over to Alphonse. He lifted his face as she approached.

"What's the matter? You look blue," Ruby said with a kind smile as she took a seat next to him.

"Hiya, Ruby."

"I heard that you were at the restaurant with everyone until pretty late last night. I thought you might be resting at home," she said, covering her mouth as she yawned.

"Are you tired?"

"Yeah. I stayed up all night on watch duty at the entrance." She nodded her head toward the stairway that climbed the side of the cliff to the top. "The bandits are getting bolder these days. They're attacking more frequently. That's why we had to strengthen the guard."

Alphonse looked up. He could make out five security guards standing by the gate at the top of the cliff path.

"That many bandits want to get in here?"

"Wisteria is the only place with any wealth in this whole region. And we're very close to the border between the Eastern Sector and the Southern Sector here. That means we border two military jurisdictions, which works in the bandits' favor. They do what they want on one side and then just cross the border to get away from the military when they come—which isn't all that often."

"I had no idea . . ."

The two sat silently for a moment.

"So," Ruby said brightly, "what about the town? You like it?"

"Yeah," Alphonse nodded. "I'm impressed with how positive everyone is. I've never met so many people with auto-mail limbs who don't consider them a curse. They're even proud of them. You don't see that very often."

Alphonse paused slightly, chewing his words. "You know," he said, "I hadn't really noticed this before I came here, but I think I've been denying who I am all this time."

"Who you are now?" Ruby asked.

"Yeah . . . I don't know. It's like I've been denying that this body is *me*. I've been so busy trying to get back the body I had before."

Ruby looked confused. "So . . . why *do* you wear that armor?"

"Well, it's . . . uh . . ." Alphonse stuttered. "It's sort of a habit—except it's not really a habit. More like a necessity. It's the only way I . . ."

He couldn't bring himself to tell her there was nothing inside the suit.

Ruby laughed. "You don't have to tell me what happened if it's that hard. You know, I think you're fine just like you are. And that armor looks really great."

"You're good at accepting things as they are, aren't you, Ruby?" Alphonse said, glad that she hadn't pressed him any further.

"That's right. What happened in the past doesn't matter now. You have to accept who you are today, and just move on."

The words sank deep into Alphonse's heart. For the first time, he found himself questioning his desperate search to get back his original body. He had been in denial for so many years, constantly unhappy with the way he was.

But the people here, Ruby and Neil and the others, they were living for tomorrow with whatever bodies they had. Instead of lamenting about their losses, they were working hard for themselves, and for others . . . and they were satisfied.

Alphonse lifted his hands and opened them slowly. With these hands, he could push that cart filled with heavy stone without fear of injury. With his armored feet, he could walk and walk without ever getting tired. There were things he could do *because* he had a body of armor. Of course, he had known this before, he just had never seen it in that light.

I could live like this, as I am now.

Of course he wanted to get back his original body, but at the same time, if he could help people with the body he had *now*, that would make him happy, too. Alphonse's hands clenched into fists.

What if he could throw out the old self, the one always looking backwards, in love with his old body? What if he could grab on to the future as he was . . . He was surprised to find how happy it made him to hear Ruby say he looked great. Alphonse looked at the girl sitting next to him.

She had probably led a hard life, too. But she had overcome the hardships. She lived a new life now.

"Ruby?"

"What?"

"If I went to the mansion, could I meet Mr. Raygen?" If Raygen had single-handedly given all the people of Wisteria hope for the future, maybe he could help Alphonse, too. Alphonse had already grown quite fond of the man, hearing all the stories of his kindness. He felt certain Raygen would help him make sense of his worries, help him overcome his own past, and maybe even give him some good advice for finding his future.

To Alphonse's surprise, Ruby frowned, her brows furrowing. "Well, it's not that simple, really. Only certain people are allowed into the mansion, and the people they know well."

"Really? So when does Mr. Raygen come out into town?"

"Well he's a busy man, so he doesn't come out that often. He comes out to talk to people who want to live here, of course . . . Is that why you wanted to talk to him?"

Alphonse shook his head. "I just thought it might be nice to talk to him."

"I see."

"And," he added, hopefully, "I don't think we can stay here very long, so I thought if I could meet him today . . ."

"Well, I'll see what I can do, but even security guards aren't allowed to just walk up and ring his doorbell without a good reason."

Ruby thought a while, then she snapped her fingers. "I know! I've got a great idea!"

"Huh? What's that?" Alphonse asked, tilting his head.

Ruby grinned and gave him a wink. "You'll see!"

Chapter Three

Unequivalent Exchange

SHORTLY BEFORE Ruby led Alphonse off to meet Raygen, Edward had set out to find the boy he had seen the previous night. In his hand he carried the white petal that had fallen on his bed.

He followed the waterway downstream, and as he drew farther away from the middle of town, the air around him grew quite cool. At the downstream end of the canyon, high cliffs blocked out the sun's light, casting a shadow that lasted all day long. Even in the middle of the day, this side of town stood quiet and empty.

It had been too dark to see this part of town the night he and Alphonse had arrived. There were houses here, too, but all of them were shoddy and run-down, not like the ones near the mansion. Some leaned to one side, others lacked doors. Some had rotted clean through in the damp, dark air.

Edward walked farther until he reached the base of the cliff. Here, the artificial waterway ended. The water flowed freely out into a rocky riverbed. The cliff that ringed the village split here, into a narrow crevasse that went back a short ways before narrowing further to a close. Water rushed into the crevasse, crashing against the base of the cliff where it flowed underground through a gap in the rock.

Edward walked until he could see the crevasse more clearly. He had thought it very narrow, but on closer inspection he found it measured nearly six feet across at its entrance. The cliff here curved slightly, making the crevasse hard to see. You could easily pass your eyes over it and not notice it at all.

Right next to the crevasse entrance, perched above the rushing water from the waterway, the boy stood, tending a small bed of flowers.

"Hello there," Edward called out.

The boy looked up, startled from his flower tending by the sudden interruption.

"Sorry, sorry. Didn't mean to scare you. I saw you from my window and wondered what you were up to out here . . ." Edward gestured with his thumb back toward the house where he was staying. He looked up the cliff. "Wow, amazing. It really is high when you see it from here."

The cliff was incredibly sheer. Edward's neck hurt just looking at it. Edward pulled his eyes away from the cliff back down to the boy. "My name's Edward. Came here just yesterday."

"I'm Leaf," the boy said quietly. He held a small red flower in his hand.

"You grow your flowers here?" Edward asked, gesturing with his head at the flower bed. Even in the shade, the patch bloomed with flowers of red, blue, yellow, and violet, a patch of bright color in the gloom at the cliff bottom.

"Yes. This kind grows well even in the shade," Leaf told him. Pulling a vase out of his pocket, he stooped down to scoop water out of the rushing waterway below. Walking back up to the flower patch, he picked a red flower and stuck it in the filled vase.

Edward stood watching him care for his flowers, when he recalled the scene in front of Ruby's house the night before. "So the town doesn't think selling flowers is a useful occupation?"

Leaf laughed sadly. "Why should they?" he sighed to Edward. "Nobody in town needs flowers. Any land with good sunlight, they use to grow crops, or they build houses for the people who earn well. Where's the room for growing flowers? Besides, everyone's so busy working, they don't have time to appreciate the simple things . . . like flowers." Leaf stooped to pick another blue flower and put it in the vase.

"I think they're pretty," Edward said, squatting down next to the boy. The flowers in the vase swayed gently in the cool breeze. The tiny blossoms were indeed quite beautiful.

"Thanks." Leaf smiled sadly. "But you can't earn a living with flowers. Even if I *could* sell them outside town, the flowers don't hold up well in the desert, and besides, people up there can grow their own flowers. Down here, well . . . flowers don't do anything for the town, they say, so I can't get paid for this. But I'm not strong enough to lift rocks, and I couldn't keep up when I tried polishing gemstones at the refinery."

Edward frowned. This was a side of the town he had not seen. It made sense: in a town with special needs like this one, stuck in the middle of an unforgiving waste as it was, the residents valued things that directly contributed to the town's welfare first. Anything else was deemed unnecessary.

Leaf lifted two thin arms. "My hands can only do what they were made to do . . . and I don't think that should be such a bad thing."

"Isn't there any other work you could do outside the refinery?"

"Oh, I could grow vegetables or carry water or clean the waterway, but other people took those jobs already." Leaf shook his head and stood, pointing across the waterway. "Back there is where I live. Back where the sun never shines, as far from the water as you can get and still be in the canyon. The people who don't earn anything wind up getting pushed off to the edges like that."

The corner of town where he pointed seemed lifeless and

quiet, a stark contrast to the hustle and bustle of the factories upriver.

"Me and the others there can't do hard labor . . . so we can't earn a good living like those folks near the mayor's place. That's why we live in such shoddy houses."

Edward nodded.

"*This* is equivalent exchange."

He's right, Edward thought. In a town that held equivalent exchange above all else, it only made sense that those who produced less received less, but here, downriver, the harsh reality of that law stared Edward square in the face.

"I can see how it would be tough to live here if you were stuck on this end of town." Edward thought back to what he had been told as he came into town. "It's amazing that no one ever leaves Wisteria."

Leaf shook his head. "Of course people leave."

"Really? But I thought I heard . . ." Edward began, when the crunching noise of something breaking drifted out from the darkened houses at the edge of town. The sound of men shouting followed immediately after.

"What language do I got to speak to get it through your head?"

"Give it here!"

Next to Edward, Leaf cried out, "Not again!" and broke into a run for the edge of town.

"H-hey!" Edward chased after him. Panting for breath,

he came to a small clearing between the tiny houses. In the middle of the clearing stood a makeshift table of half-rotted boards set across a large stone. Several cups sat on the table. Nearby, three swarthy men were shouting at some older men and youths with spindly arms. Edward counted ten people in all.

"You stole fruit from the town field, didn't you! Just because you don't make good money don't mean you can steal what's not yours!"

"We would never steal!" the oldest of the elderly men there protested. "How could you even accuse us of that?"

"You should be ashamed," growled one of the tough men. "Sitting around here all day, while we work our fingers to the bone to earn our keep."

"But we're too weak to work in the factories!" the oldest said.

"Then you don't belong here!" One of the strong men grabbed the oldest by the collar. Several of the old man's friends rushed to his aid.

"Mr. Ivans!"

Leaf ran over to the two and tugged at the arm of the one shaking the oldest. "Please, no fighting!"

"You again, Leaf?"

"Maybe we don't earn lots of money like you," Leaf said hotly, "but that doesn't mean we want more than our share! That doesn't mean we would steal! Why do you call us criminals?"

"There's jobs to be had, an' yet you don't work," the man replied. "An' if you ain't earnin' your food, you must be stealin' it!"

"Face it—you're nothin' but dead weight for Mr. Raygen to carry. You all ought to leave town!" another spat.

The strong fellow with his hand on Ivans's collar let go. "Leaf, just because you know Ruby don't mean you get a free pass around here. Find some work. You might be small, but you can at least tend to the fields. And you can afford better than these people. Why are you always taking their side? Why not move out of that rat's nest?"

"Because I can't stand it that you all came here as equals, in the same straits, and then just because you make a little more money, you start calling the rest of us 'these people.'"

Leaf might have looked weak, but he had strong opinions and, it seemed to Edward, nerves of steel. The boy stared down the hulking man in front of him. "All you talk about is kicking us out. Why not help us instead?"

"What, and ignore Mr. Raygen's whole plan? His law? Didn't he save you same as he saved all of us?"

"You do know the law, don't you!?" the man next to him growled.

"Of course I do! But not all of us are as strong as you are. Some of us are old, or sick. How can you talk about equivalent exchange in front of us when it's obvious there's a problem? Or maybe you just don't care about us?"

"Why you little—" The three men stormed at Leaf.

One reached out and knocked the rotting table off the rock, spilling the cups and their contents onto the ground. Another raised his fist.

"Hold it!" Edward butted in.

"Huh? Who're you?!"

"Was that payment for your stolen vegetables?" Edward asked coolly, thrusting a finger at the cups knocked over on the ground. "I don't think so. You don't have any proof that these people stole anything. Which means that you just knocked over those tea cups for no good reason . . . so by the law of equivalent exchange, you'd have to pay for that tea that you just spilled, am I right?"

"Who do you think you are?" The men glared suspiciously at Edward.

"Hey, it's the kid who saved Ruby the other day," one whispered.

The man closest to him snorted. "Listen, kid, you're new here, so I'll give you a warning. Hang out with this lot, and people will think you're a sluggard who doesn't want to work for an honest wage, like the rest of them."

"Thanks for the warning," Edward replied with a cold smile. "What about the tea?"

The man tossed a coin in the dirt. "There. That should do just fine. I'm out of here." The men walked off, shaking their heads.

Edward watched them leave and picked up the coin.

"They could've just apologized, but they threw money," he muttered. "Let's hear it for equivalent exchange."

Behind him, the old man named Ivans and two other people who had fallen in the scuffle were rubbing their bruises and groaning.

"I can't stay in this town any longer. I'm going to tell Mr. Raygen I'm leaving," said one of them, a man wearing a threadbare jacket and a crumpled white hat.

"I stirred up some trouble in another town. That's why I'm here. I'm not sure if I can I make do anywhere else," said another, wiping the dirt off his elbow.

"Me either . . . " Ivans echoed sadly.

"Do you have any other place to go?" the first asked him.

"We have to stay here and resist them, get them to change the law!"

"I didn't come this far only to have to start another fight. I'm going to try my hand at the refinery again," said a gaunt man nearby.

"Kett! Work in your condition, and you'll only get hurt again! Better to leave town. See about having Raygen find you a job somewhere else."

A few of the men sat, bleary-eyed, their shoulders sagging in defeat. Others were angry, fists raised, talking about making change. One of the tired-looking youths stood silently and trudged off in the direction of the factories.

Leaf left the bunch and walked toward Edward. "Thank you for helping."

"I'm not sure I did much of anything." Edward handed the money to Leaf. "Give this to the people whose tea got spilled."

"Sure thing."

They stood awhile in silence, looking at the others.

"What were they saying about having Raygen find them a place to work outside?" Edward asked.

Leaf explained, "Mr. Raygen says he watches after everyone who comes in here, so when people decide to leave, he finds them work to do in other towns. Nobody here would have anywhere to go otherwise."

"Very nice of him."

"Maybe. The people who live upstream, they think we're just excess weight, slowing down the whole town. They think he should just let us find our way on our own if we want to leave."

Edward nodded and thought awhile before asking, "What's this about you knowing Ruby?"

"We came from the same town. We both got caught up in the war, and we watched our town burn down to the ground around us. We didn't have the strength to stand up and fight, so we fled. We met Mr. Raygen before he founded Wisteria. We were some of the first to come here. But . . ."

"But?"

"All of us then, we wanted to make a town so strong it

wouldn't fall, even if there were another war. But by making it strong, we left no room for the weak . . . and if that's what happens, I'd rather not be strong at all."

Edward was silent.

"This place down here is a wonderful world," Leaf continued, "but only for the strong. If you're not strong, it's impossible to keep up." The boy sighed wearily. "Back home, whenever we would go out, like for a picnic, I would always fall behind because I was so small. I remember Ruby would always wait for me then. She would come back and hold my hand and help me along."

Edward remembered the strength in Ruby's eyes the other day. He could sense her iron will, her desire for progress at any cost. He wondered what her eyes looked like when she held Leaf's hand.

"That was a long time ago, though," Leaf said, shaking his head. "I don't think that the way of things here is all wrong, but it's certainly not right. That's what I've been trying to tell people."

Edward looked at the men dusting themselves off in the clearing behind them. It was dark in this corner of town—so dark only the people who really wanted to could even see it. When Edward lifted his eyes to look upstream, the shadows disappeared, the sun shone brighter, and the town bustled with the sound of factories. And there, at the head of it all, loomed Mr. Raygen's mansion, its white walls so brilliant in the noontime sun that Edward thought anyone standing near it would surely be blind to the far side of town.

The dark side of town.

Edward had suspected that something unsavory lurked beneath Wisteria's bright and cheery surface, but he was a little shocked at how clear the division between the light and the dark really was. He felt oddly uncomfortable, like he was staring Mr. Raygen's hypocrisy right in the face.

He knew one thing for certain: Wisteria no longer seemed a paradise.

"So this would be the bad part," Edward muttered, making a mental note to add this into his report. He just wished he could be happier about his findings.

Thinking about it, he had known all along that a town couldn't really be as good as Wisteria had seemed, but now he realized that at the same time, he had hoped it was. He and his brother had stayed at innumerable towns on their journeys. Part of him had wanted to remember Wisteria as the happiest of those stops. But now that he had seen the truth, he couldn't close his eyes to it.

"Just one more thing left," Edward said to himself. He decided that once he finished his report he would leave town as soon as he could. He had a feeling it wouldn't be long before Leaf and the others followed.

He glanced at the boy. Leaf stood apart from the wearied bunch of men, his gaze fixed on the flowers in his hand. With gentle strokes, he touched the petals with the tips of his fingers.

Edward noticed something. "Don't you have any white flowers, Leaf?"

There were many flowers in Leaf's patch, but none of them were white.

Leaf pointed upwards. "Those flowers only grow in the sunlight. So I plant them up above."

"Above?!"

Leaf pointed toward the top of the cliff above where they stood, some distance away from the main entrance to town. "I climb up the crevice there to grow them up top."

Though the steep cliff wall was pocked with many little cracks and protrusions, nothing even vaguely resembling a path stood out on its face.

"I thought there was only one entrance," Edward said. "Can you go up on this side as well?"

"If you go up the crevice. I'm light, and I'm used to it, so I can manage the climb. I don't know anyone else who could. Also, you have to know the right way."

Edward nodded, taking another look at the split in the rock wall above the waterway outlet. If you went as far into the crevasse as you could go, around the natural curve of the wall, no one in town could see you. So that's where Leaf had been growing the white flowers that drifted into his room.

"But what if you get caught? Wouldn't that be bad?" Edward asked. "If no one even wants the flowers, why take the risk?"

"I suppose you're right," Leaf admitted, "but these flowers

are important to me. I keep hoping . . . hoping she'll see the flowers and that they'll remind her of who she used to be."

Edward didn't have to be told to know who he was talking about. Leaf looked up the cliff wall. He had a far-off look in his eyes, as though he were lost in thought, remembering something deeply important to him.

"I can't keep doing this forever," Leaf said. "Maybe it's time to move on. I guess it's not unusual for people to change over the years. She probably doesn't even remember."

Edward stood awhile, wondering what the white flowers meant to Leaf, what had happened between him and Ruby, but he could not find the right way to ask. In the end, he left without saying a word.

Edward walked straight up the main road, his eyes watching a plume of steam pouring from the domed factory. As he came into the sun again, he could feel his body warming. It occurred to him that the people living out here in the sun couldn't possibly imagine how cold it was to live in the shade. It seemed so wrong . . . but how could an observer like himself hope to change things? He couldn't make the sun shine on the whole town.

"This is the problem with staying in a place too long," Edward mumbled to himself as he walked. "You come as a tourist, but give it a few days, and you'll start seeing all the dirt you thought you left behind you in the last town. I think I'm more suited for the kind of trip we were on before—just me and Al, a clear purpose, and the road ahead . . ."

Edward knew it was a selfish thing to say, but behind the words lurked Edward's frustration. He wanted to help these people, Wisteria's lost, but he did not know how. Edward headed on toward Raygen's mansion, more eager than ever to finish his business here and be done with the town. He stopped in at the house where he and Alphonse were staying, intent on bringing Alphonse along. "One thing's for sure," he muttered to himself. "I'll have even more nasty things to talk about with the colonel when we're done with this."

Edward knocked on the door, but there was no answer. He looked inside. Alphonse had not returned. "Maybe he's still helping out . . ."

Edward waited for a while, but when no one came, he resolved to head to the mansion on his own. Edward decided it was all for the best. Edward knew that his brother had grown very fond of this town in the short time they'd been here. He wasn't particularly eager to tell Alphonse what he'd seen downstream just yet. He knew Alphonse wouldn't take the news of the conditions on the shady side of town well. He'd have to tell him eventually, of course, but if he could, he preferred to delay the telling just a little longer.

Edward arrived at the gate to the mansion and looked up. The gate was closed. Through the bars he could see shrubs around the white mansion that stood in the middle of the grounds, surrounded by a high iron fence. Edward shook the gate, but it wouldn't open. His loud clanging, however, caught the attention of the guards standing in the grounds at either side of the gate.

Edward blinked. He was surprised to see guards. Issues with his law of equivalent exchange aside, Raygen seemed to all appearances a very kind man. Edward had assumed the mansion would be open to the public. He waved a hand through the gate at one of the guards.

"Excuse me!"

One of the guards walked over. "What?"

Edward blanched. The guard's gruff attitude told him he wouldn't have much chance of getting in this way, but he tried all the same. "Can you open this for me?"

"Not a chance."

Edward frowned. "Why not? I just wanna talk with Mr. Raygen."

"Sorry, kid. Only guards and their associates are allowed inside."

"So . . . I can't see him?"

"That's what it means."

"Huh." Edward thought. He could always write his report and just fill in the leadership part by guesswork. However, he knew he'd run the risk of being found out. He *could* sneak his way in with Alphonse and force the guy to talk to them . . .

He looked up. The other guard had approached and was nodding at him. Maybe he still had a chance. "You're the kid who came here yesterday, aren't you?" the guard asked, the concern plain in his voice.

Hah, Edward thought. *Here I was, thinking of fighting my way through these guards, and this guy's taking pity on me. He must think I'm some dejected child, sad that I can't meet my hero, Mr. Raygen.*

"You got lucky, meeting with him yesterday," the guard said. "Normally, he's so busy that he doesn't have much time to come out."

Edward nodded and was about to thank him when he noticed someone heading into the mansion behind the fence . . . someone very familiar.

"Al!?"

Edward grabbed the gate with both hands. Alphonse was just about to step through the door of the mansion. He turned when he heard his brother call his name. "Ed!"

Alphonse waved, and ran back toward the gate, Ruby joining him.

"Al!" Edward shouted, "How did you get in there?! Hey, guard!" He turned to one of the security guards. "That's my brother in there! We're related! Doesn't that make me an associate?! Let me in!" Edward rattled the gates.

On the other side, Ruby frowned. "Like an animal in a cage . . ."

Alphonse chuckled. It was a good description, but Ruby hadn't seen his brother at his worst yet, not by far.

Heedless of her remark, Edward kept shouting. "How did you get in there, Al! They won't let me in!"

"I haven't been inside the mansion yet myself," Alphonse replied, walking closer. "We were just about to head in to have a chat with Mr. Raygen."

"That's right." Ruby walked over and took Alphonse by the arm. "Let's be going, shall we?" she said, throwing a disparaging look at Edward.

"But I thought only guards and their associates were allowed inside?" Edward protested. Why was Alphonse getting in and not him? And something else was bothering him, too. He called out to Ruby. "Say, what's with the dress?"

Until now, he had seen Ruby only in her security outfit—camouflage trousers and a military surplus jumper—but today, for some reason, she was wearing a long, billowing skirt. And the way she was holding onto Alphonse's arm and talking so sweetly, it all seemed wrong . . .

Ruby chuckled.

"What!?" Edward frowned unconsciously at Ruby's smile. Something was terribly odd here, but he couldn't put his finger on it. This was not the Ruby he knew from the day before. He looked up at Alphonse, but Alphonse merely scratched his head.

"Actually, um . . ." his brother began.

"Actually what?"

"I'm getting in as Ruby's fiancé," Alphonse admitted.

"Whaaaaat!?"

Ruby held tighter to Alphonse's arm. "That's the only way he could get into the mansion. Alphonse likes our town so much, and he wanted to talk to Mr. Raygen, so I decided to introduce him as my fiancé. It's the least I could do for him. Isn't that right, Alphonse?"

"Pretty much." Alphonse shrugged, obviously embarrassed by the whole situation.

"That's why you're dressed like that?" Edward asked, dumbfounded.

"Just getting in the mood." Ruby smiled.

"I gotta say, you look terrible in a dress."

"How rude!"

"I don't know, Ed," Alphonse said meekly. "I think she's kinda cute."

"Really? Thank you, *Alphonse*."

Edward's eyes shot from Alphonse to Ruby, then back to Alphonse again. This whole charade had just ceased to be funny. Edward grumbled under his breath. Here he was, worried about disappointing his brother with Leaf's story . . . all while Alphonse had a ball pretending to be Ruby's fiancé.

Ruby laughed even harder at Edward's scowl. "What? Afraid I'll steal your brother away?"

"Hey!" Edward felt himself blushing, though he wasn't sure why. "No!" he blurted. "That's not it at all! I just want to get in there, too!"

"Oh, that's right, Ed. I'm sorry," Alphonse said, remembering their mission. He hastily pulled his arm away from Ruby. "Why don't you be Ruby's fiancé? I think you play the part better than me, anyway. It's hard to imagine me getting married in this suit of armor."

"No way!" shouted Edward and Ruby together.

"Me? Marry that shrimp!?" Ruby added.

"Why you . . ." Edward growled.

Ruby grabbed Alphonse's arm again, pulling him toward her. "I know Alphonse wears this armor because of what he believes in, isn't that right, Alphonse?"

"Huh?" Edward gawked at her.

"Er . . . Ruby . . ." Alphonse began, but Ruby cut him off before he could explain.

"I think it's wonderful! Why, I consider myself lucky to have gotten to you first!"

"Uh, thanks, Ruby, but . . ."

Ruby yanked Alphonse's arm, turning him back toward the mansion. She glared at Edward. "So long, brother-in-law!"

"Brother-in-what!? Hey!" Edward fumed, then stopped. He had an idea. "Okay, fine. So he's your fiancé. How about you introducing me to Mr. Raygen as your fiancé's brother?"

Ruby snorted. "Impossible. No one would believe you're his brother."

"What's that supposed to mean!? This better not have anything to do with my height!"

"Okay, okay, okay. That's probably enough of that." Alphonse said loudly, waving his hands as he stepped between the two.

"Don't stop me, Al!"

"Oh, you want to fight?" Ruby said. "No need to stop him, Alphonse. *I'll win.*"

The two continued glaring at each other through the gate when they heard a scream coming from a distance.

"What was that?" Edward asked, whirling around.

"It came from the dome!" Ruby shouted.

Alphonse flung the gates open and broke into a run in the direction of the scream. Ruby and Edward followed close behind, their argument temporarily forgotten. When they reached the dome, they found a woman standing over a man who was sitting down, his leg wrapped in a towel. Neil stood nearby.

Alphonse waved at Neil. "Is he hurt?"

"Aye. He toppled the cart," Neil replied, glancing over at one of the ore carts. It lay on its side next to a spilled load of rock and gravel. The man moaned, gripping his leg through the towel.

Edward took the towel off gently and looked at the injured leg. Blood soaked the towel, but the wound did not seem deep. The leg had begun swelling from the ankle up to the knee.

"Looks like you sprained it getting out from under those rocks," Edward said. "It should mend with two or three weeks of rest. You're lucky—the bone isn't broken." Edward clapped the man on the shoulder and looked up. No one else there seemed particularly pleased with the news of a light injury. Nor did they seem that concerned about the man. Instead they all gathered around the cart and began scooping up the spilled contents.

"I told him to give it up," Neil grumbled, sighing loudly.

The man with the wounded leg shuddered.

"He hurt himself before, you know," Neil told Alphonse. "Now he comes back saying he'll work again, and not ten minutes later, this happens. He's not earning money; he's causing all of us trouble. Useless."

The man lifted his face from his knee at the disgust in Neil's voice. "Please, Neil . . ." the man said, clutching at the big man's hand. "The cart was heavy! My hands slipped, that's all! It won't happen again, I promise!"

Edward recognized the man clinging to Neil's arm as one of the older men he'd seen downstream. He'd seen him in the clearing, promising that he would try to work again.

"Please, you have to understand, I'm a wanted man outside Wisteria. The military's after me! I can't leave. Please, let me work . . ."

Neil frowned down at the man. "If you want to help out, then go carry water or something easier like that."

"But you can't earn a living wage like that!" he cried, despairing. The man's arms slumped to the ground in defeat. His foot may have only been sprained, but his heart seemed crushed by this injury, coming so soon after his fresh start. A tear slid down his cheek and fell to the dusty ground.

As the old man softly sobbed, the sound of footsteps on

gravel came from behind them.

"I feared that scream sounded like someone I knew . . ." the newcomer began. It was Ivans. Leaf was standing beside him.

"Are you okay, Kett?" Leaf asked, kneeling next to the injured, sobbing man, and giving him his arm to lean on.

"It's just a sprain. He'll be fine in no time," Edward explained.

"I'm glad," Leaf said, though he had worry in his eyes. Next to them, Alphonse stood staring at Neil and Ivans.

"Neil," Ivans said suddenly, "maybe it's time you reconsidered this."

"Reconsidered what?" The big man raised an eyebrow.

"Determining pay based on what helps Mr. Raygen and the town might be good equivalent exchange, but there's a gap between the rich and the poor here, and it's widening. Do you want to make a true paradise here? Then we should go to Mr. Raygen, talk to him as a town. We must figure out something that's fairer to all."

Neil spat. "Fair? What's fair mean to you? You want to give people who don't work the same money as people who do? I'm sorry, but I'm not sweating fifteen hour days here for nothing. And frankly, I don't think someone earning as little as you's got the right to tell me how our town should run."

Ivans was not so easily dissuaded. "Why is it that you work fifteen hours, again? Is it to pay back Mr. Raygen for giving you a helping hand? Or do you just want more money?"

Neil frowned silently.

"This is how our town will perish, Neil. Weighed down into the ground by the law of equivalent exchange."

"Don't blame Mr. Raygen for your lack of effort!" Ruby put in suddenly. She had been quietly helping to pick up the stones that had fallen from the cart, but this last comment from Ivans had set her off. "You weren't happy with your life before, right? That's why you joined Mr. Raygen, right? To build a new world, a strong world, better than the last one. Just because you can't keep up doesn't mean Mr. Raygen's wrong. If you can't build our world, you should leave!" Ruby was furious. Her voice held the conviction of one who truly believed what she said and would hear no other views on the matter.

The crowd fell silent until Edward spoke. "Hang on. Ruby, I've got a question for you." All eyes turned toward the young alchemist.

"What?" Ruby asked suspiciously.

"Would you say the people living here in Wisteria are living, thinking people . . . or puppets, like in a puppet show?"

Ruby frowned. "They're people of course," she replied, rolling her eyes at the inane question.

Edward shook his head. "Not if they stop asking questions they aren't," he said quietly.

Ruby raised an eyebrow, not understanding, but she noticed the look of sympathy in Edward's face and it bothered her. Ruby turned and began to leave when a thin, gangly-armed boy stepped in her path.

"Leaf..."

Leaf held a colorful bouquet of flowers in his hand. Some of them were white. He held them out to her. "For you, Ruby."

Ruby favored him with a cold, withering glare. "I'm tired of telling you this, but I'll say it once more."

Alphonse looked up, startled at the lack of warmth in Ruby's voice. This was the first time he had heard her talking to Leaf. He stood next to his brother, quietly watching the two.

"Flowers don't put food on the table of anyone in this town," Ruby explained. "Why do something that doesn't help at all? Why?"

Leaf was silent.

"You remember when our village was burned to the ground?" Ruby continued. "Didn't you say you wanted to become stronger then? Didn't you say you wanted to become strong enough to live on your own? But now that you're here, where we have a chance, all you do is grow flowers and stand next to all those folks who don't want to work..." she finished with a glare at Ivans and Kett standing behind him.

"You've changed, Ruby," Leaf said sadly.

Ruby's response was cold and hard. "Yes. I'm not the little girl with tears in her eyes anymore. I made my choice. I decided to change. Why haven't you? Isn't our future worth working for?" Ruby's voice was unwavering and firm.

To Edward, who had seen firsthand the conditions downstream, this side of Ruby, her way of only seeing the good in Wisteria and ignoring the bad, set off alarm bells in his mind.

"Fine," Ruby said, relenting. "I'll take the flowers, but this is the last time." She snatched the bouquet out of his hand and, like she had the day before, plucked out the white ones and handed them back. Leaf pushed her hand away.

"I'm not growing these for the town, Ruby. I'm growing them for you. Why can't you see that?"

"What you mean? See what?"

"Don't you remember, Ruby? Don't you remember the white flowers?"

Ruby's glare faltered ever so slightly. "I said I don't need them!" she shouted, tossing the flowers to the ground. "You're the one that needs to open your eyes!"

"Ruby . . ." Alphonse began, startled at her sudden rage, but before he could speak, Ruby ran off without saying another word.

"How could you forget!?" Leaf yelled after her. "You know what happens when people don't treat each other like human beings! You saw!" The words shot out of his small body with surprising volume and echoed around the town, running along the cliffs before dying into windblown silence.

"Leaf," Edward called from behind him. "I'm sorry."

"It's too late for that," the boy said, looking down at the white flowers scattered on the ground. "She's changed. I guess we all do."

"What will you do?" Ivans asked, turning to the boy.

"I'm leaving," Leaf said, raising his face.

A look of sorrow passed over Ivans's weathered features. "Why not stick it out here, just a little longer? We might yet get our chance to voice our thoughts to Mr. Raygen, we might be able to change these laws."

"No," Leaf replied. "I won't raise my fist against Mr. Raygen. Some people have it rough here, yes, but his equivalent exchange has made some other people very happy." He thought a moment. "I suppose I just wanted Ruby to realize this wasn't perfect. I didn't want her to think this was really paradise." Leaf leaned over and helped Kett to his feet.

"Leaf, I'm leaving too," the injured man said, dusting himself off. "Let's leave together, now, today. We'll ask Mr. Raygen to find us work in another town."

Leaf nodded.

Watching the two talk, Edward had the sudden realization that he wasn't seeing something unusual for this town— many others had surely left before in the same way, and many more would leave in the days to come. Wisteria was an easy place to come to, but a hard place to stay. The rumors had it all backward. Edward looked up at the cliff walls, hearing the distant echo of the factory sounds. "They can't live down in this hole forever," he said quietly.

In the whistling wind, Edward thought he could hear the precarious balance of the town tipping.

ALPHONSE SAID NOTHING during the long walk back to their house. Inside, Edward plopped down on his bed, risking a quick glance at his brother. It was impossible to read Alphonse's expression in the unchanging armor face. But Alphonse's silence as he sat on the chair by the wall spoke volumes about the pain in his heart.

Wisteria was a new world for Alphonse: a happy town, governed by a kind man, where equivalent exchange had created a way for people to put their troubled pasts behind them and begin anew. He had even thought about joining their community. It seemed almost a dream, but reality had rudely interrupted and cut his dream to pieces. Alphonse wasn't dumb. He understood there was no such thing as a perfect place. Yet Raygen's kindness had deeply impressed him. So few people willingly took in those with nowhere else to go. Yet now he saw that Raygen's equivalent exchange had set townsperson against townsperson in the worst of ways.

In the space of a few minutes, Alphonse had gone from dreamlike fantasy to bitter understanding, and the shock was great.

Edward sat awhile, unsure of what to say. It occurred to

him that Alphonse might not want to talk at all, and so he stayed silent. Edward lay back, looking up at the ceiling, dangling his legs over the edge of the bed. After a short while, Alphonse spoke.

"Your foot . . ."

"Huh?" Edward sat up.

"Your foot," Alphonse repeated, pointing at Edward's feet where they hung off the edge of the bed.

"Oh! Sorry," Edward apologized, realizing he hadn't taken off his shoes before lying down. He sat up and began working the laces of his right shoe.

Alphonse was still staring at his foot. "You've got a blister, don't you?" he said.

"Huh? What?" Edward looked up at him. "What are you talking about?"

"Your blister," Alphonse repeated, pointing at Edward's left foot. "When we were walking in the wasteland, before coming to Wisteria, you got a blister on your foot. I know."

So Alphonse had noticed the blister. It didn't hurt anymore, thanks to the long soak. Edward hadn't even thought to mention it. Now that Alphonse had brought it up, he wondered why. Edward sat patiently and waited for his brother to continue.

"It hurt, didn't it? I know you didn't say anything, but I noticed you limping a little."

Edward thought he was walking normally by the time they had reached the town, but he must have still been unconsciously dragging his foot. Leave it to his brother to notice something like that. After years of journeying through trackless wildernesses together, Alphonse was an expert at watching his brother walk. He would have noticed a pebble in his brother's shoe before Edward did.

"Oh, right," Edward admitted. "But it doesn't hurt anymore. Don't worry about it."

Alphonse shook his head quietly. "That's not it."

Edward raised an eyebrow.

"I wasn't worried about your blister." Alphonse lifted his face and stared into his brother's eyes. "But why didn't you tell me?"

"Huh? Well, I just figured I'd grin and bear it . . . and besides, you're my little brother. I'm not going to go crying to you about every little bump on my foot . . ."

"That's not why you didn't tell me," Alphonse cut him off. "You didn't tell me 'cause you didn't want to hurt my feelings." Alphonse pointed at his own chest. "I don't get hungry. My feet don't get blisters . . . and I'm strong as an ox. Ed, if you'd just told me your foot was hurting, I could have given you a piggyback ride the whole way here. But you didn't say anything . . ."

Edward sat silently.

". . . because this isn't my real body, and you didn't want to remind me. If I had my real body, I wouldn't be able to carry you. In my real body, I'm just a kid. That's why you never complained."

Edward was the one who had affixed his brother's soul to the walking suit of armor. He knew better than anyone else that Alphonse didn't get tired, didn't feel pain, and never slept. And more than anyone else, Edward believed it was his fault.

Alphonse shook his head. "I want to get back my original body, sure I do, but why shouldn't I use this body in the meantime? When I see you holding back like that . . . it hurts." His voice held not a trace of accusation or sadness, but Edward could guess at his thoughts. He knew how tough their long search was on both of them, and Alphonse wanted to do everything he could to lessen his brother's burden. He didn't want Edward to hold back on account of his feelings— not just this time, but all the times before too.

At the same time, Alphonse had trouble offering help with his armored body, knowing how dedicated Edward was— how dedicated they both were—to getting their original bodies back. Sometimes, Alphonse even worried that, if he started relying on this new body too much, he might forget what his old self was like. That's why the townsfolk of Wisteria had impacted him so much. These people had lost limbs, family, lives, and yet they pressed on with whatever strength they still had. They kept their eyes forward, filled with pride. It made Alphonse realize how fixed he and his brother were on the past.

"I thought Mr. Raygen might understand what I'm going through. Maybe he would have good advice for me,"

Alphonse said after a long silence.

"I see now," Edward said, nodding. His brother wasn't blaming him, but he realized now the grief his words and actions had caused.

Another long silence followed. The sound of the water rushing through the waterway nearby seemed unusually loud.

"Al," Edward began hesitantly, "do you . . . do you want to stay in Wisteria?"

It wasn't an entirely unreasonable question. Alphonse had seen the bad that came from Raygen's equivalent exchange, but he had also seen the good. If he stayed here, he would be freed from the specter of his original body, free to start over with what he had now—and Edward wouldn't stop him.

He clutched his hands together, waiting for an answer.

Alphonse stood. "Ed, do you like who you are now?" He sat on the stairs next to the door, looking out at the water rushing by.

"Huh?"

"I like how I am," Alphonse continued. "If I can help people with this body of mine, that would make me happy. I think it's really great what the people of this town say, that you have to live as who you are now." Alphonse looked at his brother. "But I also heard what you said to Ruby back there, about people turning into puppets if they forget how to ask questions."

"Yeah?"

"I wanted Raygen to show me the way," Alphonse explained, "but that would just make me another puppet, following orders. What you said made me realize that. I can't just forget who I was . . . but I can accept who I am now. What I was *was* me, and what I am now is *also* me. I'm not one or the other. People aren't that simple." Alphonse's voice had the clarity of someone who had worried about something for a long time before making his decision.

"A-Al!" Edward stammered, blushing.

"Thanks, Ed. If you hadn't said that, I might have forgotten who I used to be. I mean, it is pretty nice, not getting hungry, not getting cold, not getting tired." Alphonse laughed. "About the only thing my original body has going for it is that I'm a little taller than you. But it is my body. And I do want it back."

"You jerk, you had me worried for a second there," Edward said, grinning and rapping Alphonse on the helmet with his fist. "What you said before, about me not asking you for help . . . It doesn't matter if you're a walking suit of armor or not! There's no way I'm asking my little brother for help."

"See, you shouldn't hold back like that, if I can make things easier—" Alphonse began.

"Me, go crying to you?! No way. No piggyback rides for me, even if my whole body's a giant blister!"

"Oh, I get it. This is pride," Alphonse guffawed. "How

cruel . . . Here I am trying to help out any way I can, and you won't let me." He stood and pointed a finger at his brother in mock accusation. "I'll give you a piggyback ride one of these days. Mark my words."

Edward chuckled. "Just try it! Once you get back your original body, it'll be me giving *you* that piggyback!"

"You sure you could?" Alphonse asked, putting his hand on his chin in thought. "As I recall, I was taller than you . . ."

"What difference does that make!?"

"About two inches."

"Feh."

The brothers laughed. Above them, white clouds drifted through a blue sky, sliding over the edge of the cliff and disappearing. Edward made a fist and stood in front of Alphonse. His brother made a fist of his own and placed it over his.

"We'll find a way to get back your true body, Al, but until then, enjoy what you got!"

"Roger!"

Edward stretched and yawned. "Well, guess it's about time to leave this town," he said, grabbing his traveling trunk. Now that he had seen the dirt beneath Wisteria's shiny surface, he wanted to leave at the first opportunity.

Alphonse raised a hand. "Wait, Ed."

"What? Who cares about the observation. We've done

enough. We're not getting in that mansion, anyway."

"That's not it," Alphonse said. After a moment's hesitation, he added, "Didn't you think it was strange?"

"Strange? What?"

Alphonse pointed outside, in the direction of the mansion. "How could a person as kind as Mr. Raygen be so blind to the problems his law of equivalent exchange is causing in his own town?" His gaze ran over the tightly closed gates and the wall surrounding the mansion—a perfect barrier between the people of the town and Raygen. "Why would someone open his arms to people in need and then shut them out with walls?"

"Yeah, that is strange. I don't know how important this guy thinks he is, but he does seem obsessed with privacy."

Alphonse nodded. "There's something else, that thing you said to Ruby about forgetting how to ask questions. I think you're right. Ruby and Neil have forgotten that right along with their rough past. They're so obsessed with the money they can make off equivalent exchange, they're forgetting to be human . . . the perfect loyal workers."

"Or loyal troops," Edward added.

"Exactly."

Plenty of people out in the wasteland didn't like the military these days, and it wasn't hard to imagine that some of them would want to make an ideal country, free from the military's reach. Some dissidents with wealth and charisma had even tried to usurp the military's power and required constant observation.

"Dig up lots of jewels, use the money to make a seccession state . . . this equivalent exchange could be nothing more than a convenient way to get people to stay in the town as cheap labor . . . and as soldiers."

"Maybe we should look a little deeper, see what we find?"

Alphonse was silent. Ivans and Leaf might have had it rough, but Neil and Ruby were happy here. He hesitated to destroy that. "I don't know about reporting this place to the military," he said at last. "But I do think the people of the town have the right to know the truth. How can they decide what they want to do with their lives any other way? That, and I need to know what he's about." Alphonse had been so impressed with Raygen's kindness, he hadn't thought to question it—and he knew many of the other people in town felt exactly the same way. He wanted to find out the truth for their sake, as well as his own.

"What he's about?"

"Raygen. I want to know what he's really up to, because I'm starting to worry that this two-faced town takes after its mayor."

Edward understood. "Right. I'll go with you."

"Thanks, Ed!"

Chapter Four

The Truth

THE bleached-white walls of Raygen's mansion shone in the slanting light of the sun. The outer wall drew a large semicircle around the grounds, ending in the cliff wall at both ends. The tall, sturdy wall barred all visitors, cutting the mansion off from street traffic. The only entrance was the gate in front, guarded by the watchful eyes of the security patrol.

"It's strange," Edward mused. "I mean, I understand why he'd want to protect himself from the bandits up top, but isn't that what the guards at the entrance are for? Why all the guards down here? It almost looks like he's trying to protect himself from his own people." Edward looked up at the high wall before them. "As soon as one thing seems suspicious, everything starts to seem suspicious. You can see the wall here from the town, can't you?"

Alphonse nodded.

"Let's go back toward the cliff a bit, shall we?"

Alphonse walked along until the curve of the wall hid

them from the rest of the town. They walked casually, two visitors out for an afternoon stroll. Visitors now—trespassers once they found their way in.

"That reminds me, I'm surprised that you came up with the idea of breaking in," Edward remarked, looking up at his brother. "This is a first. Usually, I'm the one that says we should break in, and you try to stop me."

Their various adventures often gave the brothers cause to infiltrate the odd home or fortress. Sometimes, they had to play a little loose with the law, but when push came to shove, Edward was always the one who shoved first. For Alphonse to beat him to suggesting criminal activity was a novel, and enjoyable, experience.

Alphonse chuckled, seeming a bit embarrassed. "Maybe we switched places? Sorry."

"Hey, don't be sorry. I kind of like the idea of being the sensible older brother who has to hold his headstrong younger brother back from charging off recklessly and getting himself into one mishap after another," Edward said with a chuckle.

Alphonse gave him a sharp jab in the ribs. "Hey! I didn't see you stopping me! In fact, it was your idea that we go in before evening. This is *your* plan."

Earlier that day, when Alphonse decided they should go find out what Raygen was up to, he suggested that they wait until nightfall and slip inside. Edward had immediately turned the idea down. "No, if he's really up to no good, there's probably evidence inside. He probably keeps a stronger guard at night, if anything," Edward reasoned. "We should go in by light of day, when he least expects it." Alphonse had agreed. After all, when it came to planning mischief, no one was better than his older brother.

The two walked until they reached the point where the wall met the cliff face. They stopped and took a look around. Edward nodded, pleased. Their position—between Raygen's wall and the back of a nearby house—shielded them perfectly from sight of the rest of the village. Edward and Alphonse looked up at the wall.

The top of the wall was dappled in the fluttering shadow of green leaves belonging to a tree on the other side.

"We could use alchemy to make a door," Edward thought aloud, "but I'm not really sure what's on the other side. Let's have a look first."

"Roger."

Alphonse made one last check to ensure no one was watching before he hoisted Edward up on his shoulders and stretched to stand on tiptoe. Balanced on his shoulders, Edward too stretched to his full height, his eyes just clearing the top of the wall.

"How's it look?" asked Alphonse from below.

"The tree's in the way. I can't see anything," came his brother's muttered reply. Edward pushed the branches away from his face to catch a glimpse of the bright, sun-drenched mansion grounds. Here and there stood bored-looking security guards. He had been wrong, it seemed. Raygen's mansion was well guarded, even during the day.

"One, two . . . five guards in all," Edward whispered down. "Plenty of cover in there, though. I bet we can pull this off."

Edward smacked the wall with his hand to check its strength, then lifted himself from his brother's shoulders to the top of the wall. Crouched in the foliage of the tree, he motioned to Alphonse, drawing a loop in the air with his thumb and forefinger.

"Okay to come up?" he whispered.

"Yeah, the tree should hide you." Edward nodded.

Alphonse took a rope and hook out of the bag at his waist and threw the end to his brother atop the wall. Edward attached the hook to a low ridge on the inside edge of the wall. The noise from the refinery near the mansion echoed around them, helping to cover any sound that they made. Alphonse climbed to the top of the wall and joined his brother in his leafy hideout. The tree's branches concealed them from both the town and the mansion.

Alphonse reached behind him to retrieve his rope when he heard the loud clang of metal crashing against metal. Someone had opened the gate in front. The two held their breath and stood perfectly still. Soon, they saw two security guards leading Leaf and Kett, the man who'd overturned the cart of rocks, who walked with the aid of a wooden walking stick. They were going into the mansion.

"They said they were leaving town," Alphonse re-membered. "They must be asking Raygen to help them find other jobs."

"They have to do something to survive."

Raygen's laws had made their life a hard one here, but it would be much harder if they left without any prospects for employment in another place. "You know," Alphonse continued, "I used to think it was awfully kind of Raygen to give them work. Now I kind of wish he'd helped them earlier, before it came to this, so they could have had a better life here." Alphonse turned his eyes downstream. "It's so bright in the sun here. You can't even see the other half of town."

Edward knew what half he meant. Earlier, Alphonse had gone downstream with him to search the rotting, abandoned houses there for rope and something to make into a hook. There, for the first time, his brother had seen a town completely unlike the Wisteria he had come to know upstream. It had been quite a shock.

"It's hard to see into the shadow when you're blinded by the light." But Alphonse knew better. He had seen the flowers that Leaf grew in the shade, and he had seen the people there, trying as hard as they could to make a living in this town that valued only the strong. It was clear that Raygen wasn't looking at the shadow. *But*, Alphonse wondered, *if he wasn't looking there, where was he looking?*

They had come here to find out just that. "Let's go, Ed,"

Alphonse said, turning back to the mansion.

Edward looked down. Beneath their tree grew a low shrub. He tensed, lowering himself to one knee on top of the wall. Alphonse crouched too, ready. They waited.

"Any moment now," Alphonse muttered, when the roof of the refinery dome began to open slowly.

"Now!" Edward hissed, together with the sound of the steam gushing from the top of the dome. The two dropped down to the ground, the clamor of Alphonse's armor lost in the hissing of the steam.

"You okay?" he asked his brother.

"Looks like we made it," Edward said, nodding.

The two crouched close to the ground and looked around. It seemed they had escaped notice. The refinery dome opened only once every few hours, but it had been worth the wait. Their plan had worked. The brothers checked out the mansion from their hiding place.

"From here, we should probably head around to the front of the mansion," Alphonse said, reviewing what he had seen of the mansion's layout from his brief trip inside the gate. "If I remember correctly, the front entrance is right in the middle of the mansion, and everything on the right and left is symmetrical."

"So it doesn't really matter which way around we go," Edward concluded, peering over the bush at the mansion. "Now, if you wanted to build an ideal country—something strong enough to stand up to the military—you'd need money first, right? Then you'd need people, and then you'd need . . ."

"Weapons," Alphonse said, finishing his sentence for him.

Yet neither could imagine a stockpile of weapons in this mansion. Though the wall was high and there were guards about, all of the curtains in the windows were wide open. The windows on the side of the mansion nearest them had been opened to let in the breeze.

"Maybe he's hiding them somewhere else?" Edward said. His eyes went down to the ground beneath his feet. "Below the ground."

"Yeah, you may be right," Alphonse nodded. "But how do we get down there? Maybe there's a way from inside?"

"Hmm. Probably." Edward looked back behind them. The ground on the other side of the mansion rose slightly, so he could see the top of the large sluice gate and the water spilling out of the cliff behind it. "Didn't Ruby say that the sluice gate divides the flow of water from the cliff into two streams, with one forming the waterway through town and the other running beneath the surface?"

Edward noted the front of the sluice gate, where the waterway diverted the water around the mansion. From there, the water flowed through numerous channels to the main waterway and into numerous smaller streams that fed the village fields. Edward's eyes ran over the sluice gate, the waterway, the mansion, and the width of the grounds, then down to the ground beneath their feet.

"If the stream really splits at the sluice gate, then that underground waterway must run right under the mansion," Edward reasoned. "If there's a cellar or some kind of storage room under the place, the river would flow right by it. They might even be connected."

Alphonse nodded. "If they had to build that underground waterway, maybe we can find the entrance they used when they were making it and go in that way."

"It's worth a shot."

Edward and Alphonse moved slowly along the inside of the wall, looking for a way below.

"Ed," Alphonse whispered to his brother, who was carefully scanning the ground in the other direction. He pointed at an iron plate set into the ground toward the back of the mansion, a short distance away. "Maybe that's it?"

The plate had turned red with rust, a square of color in the green of the grassy lawn. Edward waited for a guard to pass before leaving the safety of the shrubbery to run to the plate. Finding a small handhold in the plate's center, he thrust in his fingers and gave it a tug. "Heavy!" he grunted under his breath.

The iron plate was about three feet square and heavy as lead. Alphonse ran up to help pull. Together, they managed to lift the plate slowly from the ground.

A soft breeze blew up from below.

"Bingo!" Edward whispered. "This connects to *something*

down there." Working together, they lifted the iron plate carefully, so as not to make noise. With the plate removed, they saw a metal stair leading almost straight down into the darkness below. They slipped inside, lowering the plate behind them. The moment the entrance closed shut, the sound of the water from the sluice gate became distant, drowned by the sound of water flowing briskly below them.

After a moment, their eyes grew accustomed to the dark, and the shapes of objects came slowly into focus. Edward noticed a lantern hanging near the entrance, complete with oil and matches. Edward lit it and directed the light into the darkness below.

The staircase went almost straight down for about fifteen steps to bare earth below. The sound of water became almost deafening the deeper they went. The underground stream flowed right by the foot of the stairs.

"There's quite a lot of water going through here. Much more than in the waterway up top," Alphonse noted, coming down behind his brother. Unlike the gently flowing waterway above, its underground twin flowed at a steeper pitch, and the water rushed fast enough to carry small rocks in its flow.

The waterway was about six feet wide here. Despite the rocks they could see caught in the flow, only a few seemed to have been deposited along the bottom. *Someone must come down regularly to remove them*, Edward thought. Walkways had been built along the sides of the waterway, allowing people to walk down the tunnel. The tunnel itself, they now could see, went on for quite a distance.

"That must be the refinery up there," Alphonse said, pointing toward a beam of light stabbing into the dark tunnel some distance ahead. In the shaft of natural light, they could see ropes hanging down. These must have been the ropes Alphonse had seen used to scoop up stones in boxes for sorting.

They walked along the tunnel for a ways, looking carefully about them as they went. The builders must have tried a number of different routes for the water when constructing this place, for there were several side passages, some so narrow that only a single person could pass. With only their sense of direction to guide them, the brothers walked until they guessed they were roughly beneath the mansion. Switching to a side path, they turned several corners until the floor beneath them changed from rock to a sturdy path of wooden planks, ending in a wooden door.

"This is it." Edward handed the lantern to Alphonse and pressed his ear to the door. "Doesn't sound like anyone is in there."

Quietly opening the door, they discovered a cellar made of concrete. It was filled with weapons. The brothers walked into the room, weaving their way through countless stacks of boxes containing pistols and rifles. On the far wall hung documents describing the weapons' use, targets for shooting practice, and strategies for fighting military units, above a long stack of files along the back wall of the room. In the middle of that wall stood a wooden door, much like the one they had come through.

"I guess we found our proof," Edward said, holding a rifle up to the light of the lantern. "This is military issue. Somebody must be sneaking them supplies."

The cellar was quite large. Some of the boxes had a layer of dust on them, and others looked freshly arrived. Raygen must have been collecting these weapons secretly for months or even years. Edward expected they would find a similarly large stash of ammunition elsewhere. Their worst fears appeared confirmed: Raygen definitely planned on declaring independence. He wanted to make his little town into a nation, with the law of equivalent exchange its guiding light—and a bright and shining lure to draw in people who would serve first as labor for the town, then as its military force. The profit from the gemstones they snatched from the stream would fund their secession.

"So he *is* using the townspeople," Alphonse said sadly. "Raygen's kindness was a front . . . He doesn't really care whether the people are happy or not, in the end."

The hand of Wisteria's founder was not stretched out in kindness; he was gathering puppets to dance on his palm.

"What should we do?" Edward asked quietly. Alphonse faced away from him, staring at the weapons.

"We could tell the people of Wisteria, but I'm not sure

how much good it would do. They said they wanted a new world, after all. If Raygen wanted to start his own country, I bet many of them would choose his world over a world run by the military. Maybe some of them already know about this."

"You're probably right."

Alphonse took a rifle out of one of the stacked boxes and ran his armored fingers down the barrel. "I don't know if everyone in town would pick up one of these to build their new world, though. And . . . I'm not sure I'd have much to say to anyone who would."

Edward was silent.

"But looking at this, I know now," Alphonse continued. "I'm glad I didn't go to Raygen for advice. I can't say that the world outside is a great place, but I don't think you should destroy it to find happiness. I think you need to care for what we've already made and find happiness in that somehow." Alphonse looked at his brother. "Thank you, Ed. I'm glad you came along with me."

Edward nodded.

Alphonse waved at the crates. "As for these weapons, that's up to the townspeople to decide."

Just then, they heard the sound of footsteps behind the door across from the one through which they had entered. Edward and Alphonse exchanged quick glances, set down the weapons they had found, and went back out through the door as quickly as they could. They were halfway down the wooden-floored corridor when they heard someone step into the room they had just left.

"Maybe it's a guard?" Edward whispered, "I'm surprised they'd patrol down here."

"If we're found, they'll run us out of town for sure. Let's hurry." Alphonse turned sideways to pass through a narrow section of the corridor. Behind him, Edward scrunched his shoulders and followed. A light wavered in the hall behind them.

"Uh-oh! Al, get outside, now!" Edward hissed, handing Alphonse the lantern. Alphonse hurried off, hands clasped around the lantern so as to hide its light. Behind him, Edward ducked around a corner and hid in a side passage. Thankfully, the sound of rushing water from the main tunnel drowned out the noise of Alphonse's footsteps. The wavering light from down the hall came closer, and Edward crouched to the floor, afraid even to breathe.

He heard a voice.

"Are you sure it's not there somewhere?"

It was Ruby.

"Yeah," a man's voice replied. "Neil comes down once a week to dredge the river for stones, but the lamp he usually leaves in the entrance wasn't there today."

From the voice, Edward pegged Ruby's companion as one of the male security guards. As they spoke, light filled the narrow halls near where Edward hid. Holding his breath, he cursed himself for being so careless. It was the lamp they had stolen from the entrance that had given them away. He just hoped that they would get out of this place in one piece.

Ruby and the guard stopped at the intersection where Edward's passage joined the main tunnel to the weapon room. Ruby stopped and looked around. "I don't see any sign that anyone's broken in."

She stood so close to Edward that when she lifted her lantern, the light fell across Edward's feet. He tensed, ready for the fight that would surely come.

But the lantern stopped.

"With all the twists and turns, I'd be surprised if they got in this far," he heard the man say.

"So maybe the lamp just fell on its own into the river and got carried away?"

"Must be. Let's go back."

"Right. By the way," the man added, "those folks from downstream say they want to negotiate with Mr. Raygen. Should we bring 'em in?"

"We don't have time for that. The bandits have stepped up their attacks lately, haven't you heard? We have to deal with that first."

Ruby turned, her long hair dancing in the air directly in front of Edward's face. A stray strand tickled his nose, filling his nostrils with the smell of dust and soap.

Edward grimaced, a sneeze building behind his eyes, as he watched Ruby and the man walk away. They were out of sight before the sneeze got the best of him.

"Wachoo!"

The receding light stopped suddenly and began to grow brighter.

"What was that?"

"Who's there?!"

"Uh-oh . . ." Edward said under his breath before launching himself down the narrow hall where Alphonse had gone.

Ruby and the guard raced back into the main tunnel, but before they could discover him, Edward had disappeared down yet another side tunnel. He worried about getting lost in the maze of corridors, but being lost seemed better than being found, so he ran, taking right turns and left turns, putting as much distance between them as he could.

Ruby and the security guard seemed to have as much trouble navigating down here as he did. Soon, their footsteps were far in the distance, leaving Edward alone in the dark without a lamp.

His eyes open wide to see through the darkness, he walked, his only guide the faint light that came spilling from the sluice gate and the refinery.

Edward walked with one hand along the wall, feeling his way, when suddenly the texture of the wall changed beneath his fingertips. The cold rock of the wall suddenly gave way to something softer. It was wood.

Another door?

Edward ran his hands over the surface. From the shape

and size, it was definitely a door. He found the handle and tugged. It was locked.

Could Raygen be hiding something else down here, too?

They had already found the weapons. Maybe this room held the stockpile of ammunition. But Edward couldn't think of a reason why the room with the weapons would not be locked, while this one was. Looking around to make sure no lantern light was in sight, Edward put his hands together and used his alchemy to create a smaller door within the door. A blaze of alchemical light lit up the hall for a second, but his pursuers didn't seem to notice.

Edward pushed in the door he had created with both hands and quietly stepped through. Inside was pitch dark. Edward closed the door behind him and walked forward, waving his hands in front of him to feel his way.

"Ow!"

Edward crouched and grabbed his foot. He had run into something midstep and nearly lost his balance. He reached out until his fingers found something like a wooden box resting on the floor. He ran his thumbs across the top until he found the edge. Then, he quietly lifted the lid. Edward thrust in his hands, having an idea of what he might find, but what his fingertips touched felt nothing like the weapons they had found earlier.

He reached in and picked up a small object. It felt cold, like metal, but it was small enough to fit in the palm of his hand. The surface was smooth, though faceted. It was roughly the shape of a sphere. He reached in and found another. This one was more of an oval, with many hard edges and corners.

"Wait a minute . . ."

Edward clapped his hands together and put them on the floor. After a flash, the floor beneath the box swelled up, tipping the box on its side and spilling its contents on the ground. In the brief alchemical light, they shone like a thousand stars in the night sky.

"Jewels!"

Edward gasped. In the moment's light, he had seen box after box, each of which must have been filled with gemstones. The sight stunned him, and yet, at the same time, he had a sinking feeling that these would only be used to buy more weapons.

Still, Edward thought, *if these boxes are all full, there's an awful lot of gemstones here. Even if he's been taking them out of the town to sell, he's held quite a few back.*

Edward wondered why Raygen had hidden the gems back here, locked away, while the weapons had been relatively out in the open. He listened at the door but heard no sound of his pursuers. Ruby and the security guard must have given up or assumed that his sneeze had been just a trick of the water. Something else was odd, too. If Ruby and the guard knew about all these gemstones and expected an intruder, surely they would have come here to check. Perhaps they didn't even know this room existed.

Edward used his alchemy again and tipped over another box to find even more glistening gems. Based on his best guess at how many gemstones Wisteria collected every month and how many gemstones he saw, Edward guessed that Raygen held back as many as half or a third of the gemstones for this secret stash.

Yet something didn't add up. Raygen obviously paid some workers quite well per equivalent exchange, and accumulating all those weapons couldn't have been cheap. Yet here were all these unsold jewels. Edward sat down on one of the crates, thinking, and then he jumped to his feet with a gasp. He had just remembered the conversation he'd had with Roy when the colonel had first sent him on this miserable mission.

"What did he say about criminals?" Edward muttered to himself. Arrests had been on the rise in the southern sector, he recalled. Roy said that rapid modernization had left the factories without enough workers. Desperate managers had begun filling positions by going to human brokers who sold criminals into forced labor.

"Oh, no!"

There were many bad people in the world, Edward knew. He had met more than his share. And one thing he knew about bad people: the worse they were, the better they were at covering their tracks. They could use people up and throw them away without anyone ever knowing.

A nasty suspicion took shape in Edward's mind. It was time he and the colonel had a chat about this, and soon.

"AL!"

Alphonse turned at his brother's voice. He stood outside the wall surrounding Raygen's mansion. "Ed, you made it!"

Edward climbed back over the wall and ran up to his brother.

"They didn't catch you?"

"Or you!"

"Not yet. We got lucky. Apparently there was a bandit attack while we were inside, and all the guards got sent out." Alphonse pointed up at the cliff above. Edward could see security guards beginning to make the climb down from the entrance. It seemed the attack had been repelled.

"It sounded pretty bad up there. I heard a lot of gunfire."

Edward nodded and then suddenly broke into a run.

"Ed?" Alphonse yelled after him. "What's wrong?"

"I need to go check on something. Stay here, Al!"

"What?! Did something happen? Did they see you?" Alphonse ran hurriedly after Edward, turning around to look and make sure no guards were following them. There was no one else in sight.

Edward stopped and called back. "I didn't get found . . . but I found something."

"Huh? What?" Alphonse stood, confused.

Edward turned and ran back to his brother. "That Raygen might be a worse person than we thought," he said, panting. "I found proof. But . . . I'm not sure. I need to get outside and talk to the colonel!"

"What, now? I'll go with you!" said Alphonse, jogging alongside Edward as they returned to their house.

"No, Al, you stay here. I need you to stop anyone living downstream from going to Raygen for help."

"Why? There's nothing wrong with that, is there? If he said he could get them work, why, all of them should be asking Raygen for a way out . . . " Alphonse didn't want the people already suffering here to suffer any longer. Edward shook his head.

"No. Just, keep them from going to Raygen until I check on something with the colonel. I'll tell you everything later."

Alphonse paused and then said, "Okay." He knew Edward never made a claim unless he was absolutely sure of it. And to see him so hurried could only mean he had learned something vitally important. Even though Alphonse worried about sending Edward off through the bandit camps alone, he knew his brother wouldn't be swayed now that he'd made his decision. Besides, if anyone could take care of himself, it was his brother, Edward Elric, the Fullmetal Alchemist.

"Then, be careful. I'll do what I can here."

"Great, Al. I'll be back soon!"

Edward waved and headed up toward the entrance to the valley.

Meanwhile, Alphonse went the other direction, downstream, to stop anyone else from leaving.

Edward crossed through the central square, walking past men resting on the benches. He overheard snippets of their conversation as he passed by. They were talking about work, unsurprisingly. One spoke cheerfully about the upcoming monthly payday. It occurred to Edward that they might actually know everything that was going on here. They might be in on Raygen's plan to build a new country in defiance of the military. But seeing the innocent smiles on their faces, he knew at a glance that they did not understand the sacrifices it would take to build their ideal world.

Edward walked up the narrow, winding stairs until he stood high above town. Looking down, Edward paused in thought. *Wisteria, country of smiles. I wonder how long it will last.* Edward stopped for only a moment to take in the view. When he resumed his march, he moved much faster and more deliberately, his growing sense of unease speeding him on his way.

Inside the valley, the shadows had already deepened into evening, but up above, the sun still shone low in the desert sky. He stuck his head over the top of the cliff and was bathed in the light of the west-leaning sun.

"Whoa, bright," Edward muttered, holding up his arm to

shield his eyes. One of two guards standing nearby noticed him and turned.

"Hey," he called out. "You're Edward, right? Didn't expect to see you back up here so soon."

"I need to get to the closest town," Edward quickly replied.

"The closest town?" The two guards looked at each other.

"I can't?" Edward asked, noticing the frowns on the security guards' faces. He had worried a bit about this. A town that didn't let anyone in was unlikely to let many out, but it seemed the man's scowl was for a different reason.

"I'd advise against it—it's dangerous out there."

"The bandits are getting bolder lately."

The guard, holding a rifle with both hands, motioned out into the waste with his chin. "Bandits called in some friends. They're more confident now. They've come within range of our rifles three times in the last day."

Edward squinted, looking out over the gently sloping plain. There, in the distance, he saw them. Even at this distance, he could see the weapons in their hands. There were many more now than when he and Alphonse arrived, that much was clear. Even now, it looked as though they were on the verge of launching another attack.

"If you have to go, we won't stop you," said the guard, casting a worried look at the bandits. "We'll cover you as best we can."

"Right," said Edward, breaking into a run.

"W-wait!" the guard yelled after him. "Send us a signal if they catch you . . . and take a right by the large rock—it's a shortcut!"

Within moments, the man's voice was lost in the wind. Edward waved over his shoulder and kept running. It was tough to know how he should feel, he reflected. These guards were Raygen's men, slaves to the system of equivalent exchange that Edward knew was anything but equal. He felt sorry for them, but at the same time, he now realized that some of them probably knew the whole story. They knew about the weapons, about the coming secession from the state. They knew about Raygen's true plans.

Like Ruby.

Edward had seen enough of this crazy world to know that he couldn't save everyone. He had trouble enough making his own way sometimes. That was why he had always remained the observer. Until now. Edward bit his lip. He had seen someone offer help and give only lies. He had seen an unfair law of equivalent exchange give the strong reason to prey upon the weak. He had seen glistening gemstones turned into cold metal guns. And he had seen people in despair turned into money.

It had taken finding those gems for Edward to realize what was happening in Wisteria. He remembered what Roy had told him—that South Sector had experienced a surge in criminal arrests, that selling human labor to meet the high work demand had become a profitable business. If it were really true, if Raygen were really selling the dropouts from Wisteria to fund his new, perfect world . . .

As he ran out into the waste, Edward realized why he was running. Edward was running for the people of Wisteria—the innocents both downstream and upstream who didn't know the scope of the injustice Raygen had perpetrated upon them. Edward slapped his hands together, forming his auto-mail arm into a long, sharp blade that glowed red in the light of the setting sun. Ahead of him, the bandits waited.

Edward didn't slow down. "Out of the way!" he shouted as he cut through their midst like a sudden desert wind. He had no time to stop. For the first time in a long while, Edward had justice on his side, and it drove him on ever faster.

WHILE HIS BROTHER ran across the waste, Alphonse headed back toward the refinery dome. Downstream, he had already warned Ivans not to ask Raygen for more work. The older man had asked him why, but Alphonse could only tell him to trust Edward and wait until Edward returned. Then he had turned to go back up to the factories. He had to talk to Neil.

He found the burly man standing in front of one of the hot furnaces, his chest and arms glistening with sweat. His face glowed with the pride of a man doing tough work and doing it well. When he noticed Alphonse standing at the entrance to the dome, Neil stopped his work and walked over to him.

"Yo, Alphonse. What's up?"

Alphonse motioned for Neil to follow him and stepped outside, where the evening winds had begun to blow. He spoke slowly, reluctant to do anything that would rob Neil of his smile—but he had to tell him what they had seen below.

While Alphonse told him about the weapons, Neil stood, leaning against the dome, his face a blank mask.

"Did you know about this, Neil?" Alphonse asked, noticing the lack of surprise in the big man's face.

Neil shrugged. "I've never seen the weapons myself, but I figured they were there, somewhere. If you're going to build a new state, you will have to answer to the military at some point."

"And you still stay here?"

"Yes," Neil nodded. "I've got a bone to pick with the military myself. Truth be told, I wouldn't mind taking a shot at them. Besides," Neal said with a wry chuckle, "I've no other place to go."

Alphonse shook his head. "How can you say that?"

"What?" Neil said with a frown.

Of course, Alphonse knew Neil had no home, but before the big man could respond, Alphonse continued. "Just because Raygen saved you, you tell yourself that this is the only place left for you. But maybe it's just that you aren't looking. You're happy for what you've been given here, of course you are, but that's no reason to forget there are other ways to live. Other ways for other people . . . like Leaf and Ivans. Am I wrong?"

As he spoke, Alphonse's voice grew louder and more determined. He grew increasingly certain that what he was saying was right. "Just because some people do well here and others don't, doesn't mean you should judge them based on that alone." As he spoke, Alphonse thought about equivalent exchange, and how it made it easy for people with strength to look down on those without. It was so simple, so tempting, and yet it twisted people's hearts.

Neil stood, listening, until his mouth twisted into a scowl and his brow furrowed. "That reminds me," he said at last. "Your brother said something about people forgetting to question . . . about us being machines and all. And now you say that we don't understand Ivans and his lot. Are you saying we here at the factory are bad? Are you telling me it's wrong to work hard for an honest wage?"

"Not at all," Alphonse said, shaking his head. "I'm just saying some things can't be measured by equivalent exchange."

"What's that supposed to mean?"

"I mean . . . you have to have the heart to try to understand people who are different from you. That's all."

Neil's eyes opened wide at Alphonse's words. Then, he turned and walked back into the dome without saying another word. The refinery door closed with a loud bang, cutting off Alphonse's words, and Alphonse did not follow him inside. No matter which life Neil chose from here on, Alphonse would say no more. He had only wanted Neil to know the truth. He wanted him and the others to see what was happening, to think about what they were doing, not to become machines, their ability to think atrophied and lost. Choices were not to be given away—they were to be made by oneself.

Alphonse had his say. What Neil did with that knowledge would be his own business.

With a sigh, Alphonse turned away from the refinery dome and walked, looking up at the sky. He had liked Wisteria from the moment he arrived. To Alphonse then, no place he had ever been seemed more promising than this town filled with hope and smiles. Even now, a part of him clung to that hope.

If only I could make this a town where more people, no, where everybody could be happy.

Of course there was a limit to what he might accomplish on his own, but he had an opportunity to make some change here now, and he intended to take it. Alphonse walked into the square, heading for his house, when he stopped. There, atop the bridge that spanned the waterway running through the middle of the square, sat Ruby. She was dangling her legs over the rushing waterway, looking off into the distance. She hadn't noticed him.

"Ruby . . ." Alphonse called out softly, and Ruby turned

and smiled. He walked over, and she moved, making a space next to her on the edge of the bridge. Alphonse sat down and looked at Ruby. Her face was pale.

"You don't look so well. What's wrong?"

There were many things Alphonse wanted to ask, about the weapons in the cellar, about how much she knew of Raygen's true plans, but more than that, he worried about why she looked so blue.

A faint smile on her lips, Ruby looked down at the water rushing beneath their feet. She must have been off-duty. Instead of her usual camouflage, she wore shorts, and her long straight legs were bare down to the tips of her toes. Her shoes sat on the edge of the bridge next to her.

"It's Leaf . . ." she said after a moment.

"Yeah?"

"He's leaving. Tomorrow."

"So soon? Ruby," he began gently, "weren't you the one who told him he should leave if he couldn't keep up?"

"I know, but he's from my hometown. Sure, I got mad at him a lot, but I just feel so different now that he's leaving. I know it's wrong of me."

Even though she was still angry at Leaf, she looked lonely at the thought of him leaving. Alphonse understood. "There's nothing wrong with that. Sometimes, you just have to let things go, even if you like them."

Alphonse thought back to the house and the friends he and his brother had left behind.

"You're kind, Alphonse. I think you've seen a lot. More than I have."

"I don't think so."

"Really?"

"Well, I guess Ed and I have been through a lot."

"A lot, see?" Ruby stretched her hand behind her and leaned back. She turned her head to look up at the sky. "I've been through a lot too. My hometown got caught up in the war. We both left the night we lost our families. I was so young when it happened, and Leaf, he was even younger than I was. The military said it would protect the people, but in the end, they took our house from us. I couldn't accept it. I didn't know what to do, but I decided I had to live, so I looked for work. Most people turned me away. They all thought, 'What work can a child do?' And sometimes, when I thought I'd found work, it turned out to be a lie. Yes, I have seen a lot. I was dirty and starving, and no one helped me."

Bitterness had crept into her voice as she gave her quiet confession. "And after all that, the only one who held out a hand to me was Mr. Raygen. He was like a god to Leaf and me. That's why I wanted to help build Wisteria. I wanted to repay him for saving me."

"I see . . ."

Regardless of his motivations, Raygen had helped a lost boy and girl find their way. Alphonse did not know what to think. Ruby continued, "But Leaf, he forgot how much he owed Mr. Raygen. He turned against him. I kept hoping he would understand, that he would come around. Instead, he kept growing those flowers of his, and now he's leaving . . ."

Ruby could not understand how anyone who had been through what she and Leaf had could ever turn his back on Mr. Raygen, and it made her mad.

"That's right, Ruby. You never took the white flowers Leaf grew for you. Don't you like them?"

"Raygen told us something the day he rescued us. He said, 'Never let yourself be trapped in someone else's world. Never let them choose the color of your life. Choose your own colors. Choose your own life.' That's why he likes such bright, bold colors. He doesn't like white."

Alphonse understood how much Ruby had tied herself to Raygen. Her voice, which had been low and wavering before, became bright and energetic when talking about Raygen. To Ruby, who had once lost all hope in the world, Raygen meant everything.

"So that's why you don't like white?"

"Yes."

"I know it doesn't have much color, but I still think those white flowers are very pretty." Looking at them again, he found that he really did think they were beautiful. "What's your favorite color, really, Ruby?"

Ruby said nothing.

The sounds of laughter from the restaurant echoed

around the square, and the sound of rushing water from the waterway below swept across them. They sat in silence, looking up at the starry night sky. Framed by the edge of the cliff, the night sky sparkled, and the night breeze brushed gently against their cheeks.

Aside from a few dim lights in the nearby buildings, moonlight cast a pale light upon the town.

"It's beautiful," Alphonse said. Ruby nodded.

"Yes. Leaf is stupid to want to leave. If he just worked at it, he could be happy here, I just know it."

"But," Alphonse replied as gently as he could, "what about the people who can't keep up with the way of life here?"

Ruby's replied without hesitation. "Then they have to leave."

"Is that how he weeds people out, leaving only those faithful to him, to make a loyal nation?"

Ruby looked at Alphonse, shock in her face. Her expression soon changed to bitterness. She realized then that it was Edward and Alphonse who had broken in earlier that day.

"You saw them," she said quietly. It was not a question.

Alphonse nodded. "I did."

"We're not happy with the military. Is it wrong to want to make a country where we can be happy?" she said, challenging him.

"I don't know what's wrong," Alphonse replied quietly.

"The military must have seized power from someone who came before them, I'm sure. But, if you build a whole country based on hating the military, isn't that the same thing? Would you want to live in a place like that?"

Ruby trembled with rage. "Mr. Raygen's not like that! He wants to build a country free from all the problems the military created! He wants a country of people who work together, a strong country that would never lose, not to anyone. That's why anyone who can't keep up . . ."

"But a country for which people? The ones who do what Raygen says, right?" Alphonse shot back. "If you cut away everyone who disagrees with you, don't you know what you will become in the end? There will be no one left!"

Ruby stood up. "You don't know what you're talking about!"

She had hoped Alphonse at least would understand her. She stood there, tears welling up in her eyes.

Suddenly, the sound of gunfire cut through the night air. Bandits. Ruby glanced up at the entranceway but decided the guards could handle it. She had grown used to the sound of gunfire. She turned her glare back on Alphonse.

Just as she was about to speak, an incredible explosion rocked the valley. Flames leapt at the top of the cliff. Seconds later, a rain of gravel came falling down on the town of Wisteria. It signaled the start of a clash unlike any that had come before.

THE COINS CLINKED and clanked down the insides of the phone as Edward picked up the receiver. The next moment he lowered it, thrusting an arm out to one side to catch himself from toppling over.

I haven't run like that in a long time.

Edward gasped a lungful of crisp morning air as he dialed. He stood in the telephone box of the town they had left several days before. The shortcut had brought him here in a fraction of the time it had taken him and Alphonse before, but doing it all at once—and running—had almost been more than he could take.

After a series of clicks and whirs, a military operator came on the line. Edward read off his code name and asked for Roy in Eastern Command. After a few more clicks and an ominous silence, someone picked up the phone.

"Colonel Mustang?"

". . . Speaking." From the sound of his voice, the colonel had just woken up.

Edward felt pretty sure he had been connected to the phone in Roy's office at Eastern Command, which meant only one thing: Roy had been napping on the job. His schedule hadn't improved since Edward had left, it seemed. He heard Roy yawn deeply on the other end of the phone.

"What is it, Elric? Finish your observation of Wisteria?"

"I wish. Look, I didn't want to do this job in the first place, but now that I've gone and done it, well, we have a problem. Actually, a few problems."

"Problems?" said Roy. In a flash, the sleep had vanished from Roy's voice, and he was all business. "What happened?"

"There's something I wanted to check with you. You told me that criminal arrests had gone up in the southern sector, right? First of all, I was wondering if you had any data on where those arrests had taken place."

As he spoke, Edward heard the scribbling of Roy's pen as he furiously took notes. Edward waited for the sound of pen on paper to end before he began again. "Also, about the labor shortage you mentioned. Didn't you say something about human brokers, selling cheap labor? Do you have anything more on that? Anything?"

"Right," Roy replied. "Give me ten minutes. I want to check on some things. Call me back, all right?"

"Roger."

From the time of his early morning call, Roy must have guessed that Edward was in a hurry. Edward found himself feeling an unusual gratitude toward Roy for agreeing to look into things without complaining or questioning him. He called ten minutes later. Roy told him what he had found, his voice tense.

"Most of the arrests took place on the border between our jurisdiction and Southern's. Oh, another thing: all of the arrests, without exception, were thanks to an informant. Apparently, someone made quite a lot of cash on the bounty. And here's something interesting: the informant sent his letters from the town where you are now."

"Can you tell me when the last one was sent?"

"Looks like the twelfth and the twenty-sixth of last month . . . oh, wait, there was one only two days ago. And about the human brokers, a few have been quite active in the sector, all in that same borderlands area. In other words, all of them are from somewhere near Wisteria, where you are. And here's some good news: we picked up one of the brokers for an unrelated crime just yesterday. He confessed to buying people from a certain town. I don't have all the details yet, but when I looked further, I realized that Wisteria seemed as likely as anywhere. This what you needed to hear?"

The information Roy had gathered more than convinced Edward of his suspicions. "Yeah, Colonel," Edward replied darkly. "When I put what you just said up against what I already know, it paints a pretty scary picture. I have your man. The one behind this is definitely the mayor of Wisteria. He's a crafty one, too. Move too quickly, and he's likely to make a run for it. I'll need some men."

"You got it," Roy replied without hesitation. "Our hands were tied because of jurisdiction issues, but we've contacted Southern. We're sharing information on Wisteria now. Once we've gone through all the necessary motions, I'll send some people from the nearest base."

At the same time that his suspicion became conviction, Edward began to worry about Leaf. If he had been sold to a broker, he might be lost again—this time forever. "Thanks,"

Edward replied. "I'm going back to Wisteria. I'll leave the rest to you!"

Edward set down the receiver and ran out of the booth. Raygen was obviously out of control. He had to be stopped before there was even one more victim.

EDWARD RAN BACK as fast as he could, only pausing occasionally to rest. Even so, it was well after dark when he arrived near Wisteria. The day's long exertion left him so tired he could barely stand.

"Huh?" Edward looked up. Something was wrong with the night sky. It took him a while to realize what he was seeing: thick, black smoke. "What's happened?" Edward's heart raced, and he picked up his pace. When he reached the place where he had fought with the bandits before, no one was there.

A shot rang out in the night. Edward ran for Wisteria as fast as he could, realizing what it must mean: the town was under attack. Running up the gentle slope, he reached the edge of the chasm where security guards with sticks and rifles were locked in combat with the bandits.

Several guards and bandits lay on the ground, moaning. The defenders looked like they were holding, but it had been a hard-fought battle.

Edward gave up on getting into the village from the front entrance. He returned to where the bandits had pitched their tents and found a rope and a short iron bar among the supplies left behind. Then, crouching low so he would not be seen, he headed for the edge of the cliff on the far side of town. The bandits were too preoccupied with their assault to notice him.

Edward thrust the iron pole into the ground, and with his auto-mail left leg, he kicked it down hard. Next, he tied a rope around the half-buried pole. He gripped it in one hand and looked over the edge of the cliff down at Wisteria.

By the lights of the town, he could see people standing, looking worriedly up at the entrance. They were a long way below. But with only a moment's hesitation, Edward leapt over the edge of the cliff, the rope held firmly in his right hand. The rope buzzed with the friction, and a faint burning smell filled the air, but Edward's right hand felt no heat. He fell farther, bringing his other hand up. There was a flash of light, and the rope grew longer, stretched by alchemy. Moments later, at the rope's new end, Edward dropped the last few feet to the ground.

Shaking his right hand to cool it, Edward jumped and yanked on the rope. It snapped near the top and fell down in a coil at his feet, ensuring that the bandits would not be following him. As soon as he had dusted himself off, Edward ran for the central square. The sound of gunshots echoed through the town, and many of the residents were standing by the fields or in front of their houses with worried looks on their faces.

Edward looked in the direction of the factory and the

refinery dome from the bridge over the waterway. There, too, several people had stopped work and stood staring up at the cliff.

Passing through the square, and running out onto the road toward the town exit, he ran into Alphonse. He was arguing with Ruby in the middle of the road.

"There are plenty of guards at the mansion! Why go there? You need to help people get out of here!"

"No, the guards up above will stop them. Everything is going to be fine."

"Ruby!"

Edward, relieved to see that Alphonse was all right, ran toward the two. "Al!"

"Ed!"

From the sound of his voice, it was clear that Alphonse had been worried, too. When Alphonse turned to greet his brother, however, Ruby slipped away and began to run toward the mansion. Alphonse let her go and ran up to Edward. "The attack has been going on since last night. The guards are doing all that they can, but it's looking grim."

"I had no idea," Edward replied. He told Alphonse all he had learned about Raygen and that he'd been selling his own people to brokers. Alphonse was so surprised he could hardly speak for a moment. Then it struck him, as swiftly as it had struck his brother: "Leaf!"

"That's why I came back so fast. Has he already left?"

"I heard he was leaving today, but since the attacks began,

I've been down here with the wounded helping out, so I can't say where he is for sure . . ."

Edward slapped him on the arm. "I wouldn't worry. I don't think he could get out of here with all the fighting going on. He must be hiding somewhere in town. But what about the others? Shouldn't we be thinking about evacuating?"

Edward looked around, noticing that all of the towns-people were standing still, watching the events unfold above them. Hadn't anyone considered escape?

Alphonse nodded. "I worried the same thing, but the guards are too busy defending the cliff top and the mansion. The same with Ruby . . . I thought I might make a staircase in another part of town, but all of the crags in the cliff wall make it difficult to create something straight and sturdy."

"Right. But if the bandits should come into town, there's bound to be bloodshed. And we have to find Leaf. Let's go downstream and ask Ivans if there's any other place for the people to go."

"Right on!"

The brothers headed downstream as fast as they could, where they found Ivans and Kett and several others looking uneasily up at the cliffs.

"Mr. Ivans!"

Ivans turned and favored them with a smile. "Ah, it's Edward and Alphonse."

"Have you seen Leaf?" Edward asked hurriedly. "Isn't he with you?"

Kett, sitting with his wooden staff across his knees, shook his head slowly. "He came back here with me last night, but I haven't seen him since."

Edward frowned.

"I'm sorry that this should be your welcome to Wisteria," Ivans called out from where he sat, perched on the rubble of an old house that had fallen down and never been rebuilt. "We've had attacks in the past, but never on this scale. I'm afraid it's only a matter of time before they break through. I had hoped at least you would escape . . ."

"What are you saying?" Alphonse said, walking over to Ivans and putting his hand on the man's shoulder. "When we leave, we'll all leave together. Please, don't give up. It's not over yet."

"That's right, Mr. Ivans," Edward put in. "We have to think about escape for all of us. That's why I came here: to ask you if you know any way out of Wisteria or any place where we might take shelter."

Ivans shook his head and sighed. "Not a one."

"Not a single one?"

"Only the entrance, where the bandits are now. That's the only way out."

Edward frowned. Ivans was right. It was only a matter of time before the town fell. Even if they used the weapons from the hidden stash, the townspeople stood little chance of defending themselves against the combat-hardened bandits. Nor would Roy's reinforcements make it here on time. With each tick of the clock, Wisteria fell deeper and deeper into danger.

"What should we do?" Edward muttered, half to himself, when he noticed that there were far fewer people from downstream here than he had seen before. "Mr. Ivans," he asked, "where is everybody else?"

"Oh, most of them headed for Mr. Raygen's mansion just a moment before you arrived. They want to try to convince him to negotiate, instead of shutting off the village forever."

"Negotiation sounds like a great idea," Edward said, looking up at the cliff. The sounds of gunfire had died down, but in its place, he could hear the telltale soft thuds and shouts of a brawl. The bandits were closer than ever. They had come here for the town's jewels. Instead of putting all the people in town at risk, it made sense to cut a deal, give them what they asked for, and secure the town's peace. But Edward had a sinking feeling that the time for negotiation had passed.

While Edward sat, mulling over their options, Alphonse stood and pointed toward the mansion. "Hey, Ed, maybe we should go to the mansion. If nothing else, it has high walls. It would be much easier than defending the whole town. Everyone would be safer in there."

Edward looked around. The mansion *did* look a bit like a fortress, with its encircling wall and that cliff face at its back.

"Good idea," Edward said to his brother. Then the two

called out to Ivans and the rest of the people there. Eventually, all agreed, and they set out for the mansion, picking up more people from the town as they went.

As Ivans had indicated, a large number of people from downstream were already there. They stood in front of the gate, calling out for Raygen to appear. "If you really care for your town," one older man shouted, "come out and negotiate!"

Another small bunch chanted "Keep your town safe!" over and over.

Off to the side, Neil and a number of other people from the factory had come to join the noisy mob. They were shouting for the guards to escort Raygen to safety. "He saved us once! It's the least we can do to save him now!" Neil yelled above the heads of the crowd.

It seemed that Raygen heard neither of their pleas, for the gates to the mansion remained firmly shut. The guards on the other side smiled reassuringly at Neil's bunch as if to suggest there wasn't a problem. To the others, they raised their rifles menacingly. Yet they said not a word, standing their ground behind the gate in silence.

Edward and Alphonse joined the crowd shouting before the gate. "It's too dangerous in town. There's no place to escape!" Edward yelled.

"We need the protection of your walls!" Alphonse added. "Please, open the gate!"

"Are you crazy?" Neil shouted, turning to look at the new

arrivals. "We have to get Mr. Raygen to safety first!"

Edward opened his mouth to respond and froze.

His eye caught something on the ground, just on the other side of the gate. It was a white flower petal.

"Leaf! He's inside," Edward whispered. Then he ran over to Neil and slapped him on the shoulder. "Hey!"

"Huh?" Neil said, flustered. "What do you want, kid?"

"Look," Edward said, pointing through the gate at the mansion grounds. "It's one of Leaf's flowers! Did you see him go in? Do you know when he went in?"

"Leaf?" Neal said, blinking. "Ah, I think he was tending to the wounded, but then he left and went to the mansion. Mr. Raygen had called him in. Something about finding him a new job."

"Al!" Edward shouted, turning back. Alphonse had been listening too, and he had the same thought as his brother.

"There may be a way out from inside!"

"Yeah," Edward said, nodding, I'll get the townspeople together!"

Edward left the mob in front of the gates, and ran like a jackrabbit, shouting to the people who remained in town.

He was certain that Raygen intended to sell Leaf and Kett. They were his meal ticket, and he was taking one of them with him. He had surely been planning on handing Kett, with his criminal record, over to the military, and Leaf, he could sell into forced labor. He may have already cut a deal with a broker.

If that were the case, then he would try to get at least one of his precious commodities to them. Human brokers were a despicable bunch, many of them belonging to organized crime. They wouldn't take the trifling matter of a bandit attack on Wisteria as an excuse for a missed handoff of goods. They might have forced Raygen's hand, sending him out a secret exit to make the trade.

ALPHONSE, still by the gate, was pleading with the guards to let the gathered people inside. With his strength, he could have forced the gate open, but he feared the rifles the guards held. He worried that they might turn them on the townspeople. He couldn't force his way through this gate, not without considerable risk.

"Please, open up! We must get everyone to safety!"

It was not the silent guards who replied, but Ruby. "No," she said simply from the other side of the gate. Like the guards, her expression was blank.

"Ruby . . ."

"We can't open the gate."

"Ruby, there must be a way out through the mansion! Where is it? You must let us use it!"

"If there is a way out, then get Mr. Raygen to safety first!" Neil shouted at his side.

"Neil!" Alphonse shouted, the frustration clear in his voice.

The big man frowned. "You might want to leave town, to

get on with your journey or whatever, but the rest of us, we owe Mr. Raygen our lives. He has to make it through this!"

Ruby spoke next, her eyes fixed on Alphonse. "It's like Neil says. Besides, if all the townspeople tried to escape at once, the bandits would notice, and Mr. Raygen would surely be caught. If we want to make a new world, truly, then we must protect Mr. Raygen at all costs."

Alphonse clenched his fists in frustration. From the way they talked, they sounded like Mr. Raygen's life was somehow worth more than any of theirs. It made him angry, and at the same time, sad. "Ruby, please, open the gate! You have to think this through."

Ruby took a step closer and whispered. "I think you're the one who needs to think things through."

Alphonse was taken aback. He could see the pleading in Ruby's eyes. She desperately wanted him to understand how she felt. No, she wanted more than that. She wanted Alphonse to join her.

"Let's make a new world, Alphonse—together. We can forget the past. We can start things over."

Alphonse realized how much Ruby liked him. She was inviting him to join their lives. After the argument the other day, she hadn't given him the slightest smile, but still, she wanted desperately for him to see things the way she did.

Alphonse had feelings for her too. She was strong and bright, burning with an inner fire that gave energy to everything she did and said. He liked that about her, and he didn't want to throw all that away. But now that it came to it, all Alphonse could do was shake his head.

"I'm sorry, I can't go with you. I can't forget everything. I can't live in your new world."

"You're just clinging to the past," Ruby said desperately. "That won't get you anywhere. That's . . . That's nothing but weakness."

"Maybe it is," Alphonse admitted. "But no matter how much I have to go through, no matter how much I have to suffer, I want my old body back."

Ruby listened silently to Alphonse, and then she sighed. "I'll open the gate after Mr. Raygen is safe."

"Ruby!"

"Good-bye, Alphonse." Ruby's eyes closed sadly, and she turned around and walked away. Alphonse watched her until she disappeared inside the mansion. She had left him no choice. He prepared himself to knock down the gate, security guards and all.

Just then, Edward returned with many of the townspeople in tow. "Al!" He reached the gate and pointed inside at the mansion. "Someone saw Leaf going inside with Mr. Raygen! And get this: they were with a suspicious-looking stranger in a black suit!"

"So, there *is* a secret entrance!"

Alphonse had been thinking about Ruby, but he shook

those thoughts out of his mind. They had to get the townspeople to safety, and now it looked like they had a way to do it. "Great!"

Just then there was the sound of a large explosion from above. The entire crowd looked up as one. The bandits had broken through the defenses. They were on their way down into town.

"They're coming!" one of the guards inside the gates shouted to the others.

"They're not going to mess up our town and get away with it!" growled Neil. He turned to run toward the entrance, but Alphonse grabbed his arm in a firm grasp.

"No, Neil! You can't win this!"

"How can you know that?"

"There's too many of them! You'll get hurt—or killed! We have to escape while we still can!"

Scared by the bandits, the guards inside the gate had disappeared. Edward shaped his right arm into a blade and cut away the bars holding the gate shut. "Everyone inside, now!" As he shouted, Edward used his alchemy to fix the lock, so he could close the gate behind them.

Seeing the bandits making their way down the stairs into town behind them, Alphonse and Neil pushed their way inside the mansion. Just then, they saw the guards who had survived the fight at the cliff top come running into the street behind.

"Quickly, inside!" Edward and Alphonse shouted to them. They waited until the last person had made it onto the mansion grounds, then Edward shut the gate and locked it. Next to him, Alphonse drew an alchemical circle before the gate, and, using the earth from the mansion grounds, he raised a wall higher than the gate itself directly behind it. Edward put his hands together and slapped his palms onto the high wall encircling the mansion, causing the earth beneath it to buckle and raise the wall even higher than before.

"That should hold them awhile," Alphonse said.

"Right," his brother replied, wiping the sweat from his brow. "I'll go find Leaf."

"And I'll take everyone down into the waterway tunnels."

Their purpose clear, Edward charged headlong into the mansion, while Alphonse ran for the iron door they had used the day before, yelling for the townspeople to follow. They were running out of time.

Chapter Five

The Valley of White Petals

THE INSIDE of the mansion was strangely quiet. While the grounds outside were well manned, there seemed to be no guards inside the mansion itself. After Raygen had disappeared into the mansion, the line of command had become confused. The guards didn't stop the townspeople from coming inside the grounds, and they stood aside when Alphonse went to help everyone into the underground waterway tunnels.

No one stopped Edward, but neither did they move. They still seemed dedicated to seeing Raygen escape first. The guards dutifully stood watch around the mansion grounds, waiting for Raygen to appear again and give them orders.

Edward got into the mansion without incident, and walked along corridors connecting vast rooms, eventually reaching the second floor. Looking down from a second-floor window, he could see Alphonse holding up the iron plate that covered the entrance to the underground waterway tunnels, helping the townsfolk escape.

Above all else, the bandits wanted the gems. The doors of the factory and refinery dome had already been opened and the remaining stones stolen. After they finished searching the outlying buildings, the bandits would surely turn their attention to the mansion.

Edward knew he had to hurry, but he stopped and looked across the town, downstream. Fires here and there lit the town with a flickering glow. But despite the light of the flames, he could see nothing in the darkness of the downstream half of town.

"Not that Raygen would do anything even if he could . . ." Edward muttered.

Edward had known a lot of nasty people in his day, but Raygen had to be one of the nastiest. Even humans were considered fair game in Raygen's idea of equivalent exchange. He had to be stopped.

But Edward had other worries right now. One of the townsfolk had seen Leaf through a window on the third floor of the mansion. Edward made a fist and, on the stairwell of the third floor, pressed his body to the wall and listened.

He heard a faint voice talking.

Edward stepped silently down the corridor, stopping in front of a room.

"Then I leave him in your care," Raygen said in a low, smooth voice, devoid of real warmth. It was hard to imagine that this voice of cunning and flattery he was using to assuage the black marketeers belonged to the same man who had spoken to the townspeople with such convincing sincerity. Clearly, Raygen was worried about what effect the bandits' assault was having on his guest.

"Frankly, Mr. Raygen, I'm a little concerned," another, more sinister voice said. "With your town under attack, I suspect we won't be getting any more 'help' from you. It's too bad, really. We rather liked that this place was far from . . . military eyes." *This must be his contact with the brokers,* Edward thought.

"Not at all, not at all," Raygen protested. "My loyal subjects will gladly rebuild, and even if they can't, I can make a new town elsewhere. Of course, with both the people and the gems here, I won't give it up lightly."

"Excuse me, Mr. Raygen?" Leaf's small voice interrupted. "What are you talking about?"

He probably didn't understand the conversation unfolding before him. His voice was quaking.

The door was open a crack. Edward put his face up to it, noting the positions of everyone in the room, and put his hand on the doorknob.

"So, I'll be leaving before the bandits get inside the mansion."

"I expect payment as usual, of course," Mr. Raygen said.

"Of course. You, come!"

Leaf yelped in pain as the broker yanked his arm.

Edward flung both doors open and charged the man in a black suit holding Leaf's arm, knocking his hand away.

"Hey, who is this?!"

"Wait, I know you," Raygen spluttered, flustered at the sudden intrusion. The overweight broker, separated from his prize, ran past Edward.

The broker seemed to understand the situation more quickly than Mr. Raygen did. He immediately drew a pistol from his breast pocket.

Alone, Edward could have jumped and sliced the gun in half, but with Leaf to protect, his options were limited. Edward put Leaf behind him and clapped his hands together fiercely. Then, he touched the wall behind Leaf. Raygen ran out of the room in that instant, but Edward knew he had to fight the broker first. He pulled his hand away from the wall.

Alchemical sparks flew. When they disappeared, a long pole came jutting out of the wall.

"What? An alchemist!?"

The man dodged the pole by a hair and lifted his pistol, but before his finger could press the trigger, a lump of floor swelled up before him, bringing the carpet with it, and smacked into the ceiling.

"H-hey!!"

The carpet blocked off his vision. Two seconds later, Edward nimbly sprung around the carpeted wall and threw himself at the flustered man. His fist impacted the man's face with a wet, meaty slap. The man sprawled out on the ground, his gun skittering across the room to clatter in the corner.

"Wow!" Leaf was stunned.

Edward ran over to the boy. "Are you okay?"

"Yes, thank you."

Leaf turned and looked out the window at the pillaging of the town.

"What about the others?"

"They've gone underground, to the waterway for now. But we think there's a way to get out of Wisteria from this mansion."

Edward crouched before the man sprawled on the ground and slapped his cheek sharply. "Hey, sleepyhead! Wake up!"

The man groaned. Edward continued to slap his ruddy cheek until his eyes opened. Edward dragged him up by his collar. "How did you get into Wisteria? If there's a way out, tell me!" With his auto-mail right arm, Edward grabbed the man by the throat. The man raised his hands. "Wait, I'll talk! I'll talk! Ouch!"

"So, there is a way out?"

The man must have been afraid of Edward's startling use of alchemy. He nodded furiously and pointed down. "It's underground. There's a way out. South, following the underground river."

"I've been down there. It's a maze. Which way do we go?"

"You head downstream, and you keep going. There's a

place where the tunnel meets the underground river. The tunnel gets wider there, and you'll see a number of side tunnels. Take the one on the right. It's an old mining shaft."

Edward pushed the man up against the wall and used his alchemy to wrap the wall around him, binding him tight.

"Wait there. Your military escort will be by shortly to pick you up."

Edward took Leaf back down the staircase and out to the entrance of the underground waterway. "Leaf, you heard what that man said, right?"

"Yes."

"I'm going after Raygen. I want you to go find Al and the rest down in the waterway. You tell them how to get out and get everyone outside the village."

Edward lifted the iron plate and motioned to Leaf with his eyes. "The townspeople are down there somewhere. Once you reach the bottom, just call out, and you're sure to find them. I'll follow as soon as I can, okay?"

"Okay!"

Edward made sure Leaf made it down and then slowly lowered the cover.

Edward stood and looked around.

Beyond the wall, he could hear the exultant shouts of bandits who had found gems. Some were still trying to get into the mansion. He heard them banging on the gate on the other side of Alphonse's hastily erected wall.

The guards who had been waiting for Raygen apparently

decided that it was too dangerous: they too had disappeared, either into the waterway or off into town to fend for themselves.

"I'd better catch this guy and get out of here myself."

Edward assumed Raygen had retreated to one of his weapon caches in the mansion's cellar. In order to head him off, he ran back into the mansion and opened one of the doors to the side of the central staircase. Through the door was a large hall, with six columns running all the way to the ceiling. He checked the other door and saw that it led to a similar hall. Edward noticed another door across the room beyond the pillars. That probably led to the back of the mansion, with a view of the sluice gate.

"Where's the cellar?"

Edward scanned the walls carefully and spotted a small door off to one side. Each wing of the mansion was symmetrical with the sole exception of this one door—it had no mirror on the opposite wall. He ran up to the door and put his ear to it.

He could hear the faint sound of wind blowing from the other side. "Gotcha!"

Edward opened the door. Inside, he saw a small room with a staircase descending underground. At the top of the stairs stood Raygen, about to make his escape into the cellar.

Raygen froze and turned when Edward opened the door.

"You're not getting away!" Edward shouted.

"You again!"

Raygen spun and started down the stairs, but Edward stopped him. "You're finished! In a few more hours, the military will be here. You're a very popular man. See, both Southern Sector and Eastern Sector want to be the ones to get you first. You better give up now!"

"What!?" Raygen's eyes stared, wide with shock. Clearly, he hadn't suspected that the military was onto him. "How?! Who reported me? You?!"

Edward stared Raygen straight in the face. "You know, I don't really care about your perfect country, your dreams of secession, or any of that. You gave the people in this town a little hope, once. But then you did something wrong. You sold people for money!"

Raygen seemed startled, but said nothing.

"You made equivalent exchange a law," Edward continued, "and you pushed it to the point of insanity. You promised to find anyone who didn't fit in Wisteria a job somewhere else. But that wasn't the only exchange you offered. You exchanged innocents for money. Then, you turned over anyone with a bounty on his head to the military."

Raygen listened to Edward in silence, but then an evil grin broke across his face. "You've done some homework, haven't you?"

"If you'd stuck to using your gems to buy weapons, I might never have noticed."

Raygen laughed—a deep, genuine laugh that sent chills

down Edward's spine. "Times change, but the value of gems does not. I'll have plenty of opportunities to spend them in the future. But people, they're different. You have to use them whenever you get the chance."

The full extent of Raygen's madness stood completely revealed. Edward unconsciously balled his hands into fists. He felt the bile rise in his stomach. "You're despicable."

Raygen chuckled. "Yes, but there are those who think I'm a god."

When Raygen stopped talking, Edward heard light footsteps approaching.

"Mr. Raygen, sorry to keep you waiting! We can use the entrance above. We have to go down to—Edward?!"

It was Ruby.

She had been searching for Raygen's escape route. Her forehead was beaded with sweat.

"Ruby, this man may have saved your life, but in reality, he wants to frame me for crimes I did not commit." Raygen's evil grin had disappeared. He spoke in a cool, calm voice.

"What? What are you talking about!" Edward said, disgusted, but Ruby looked more and more suspicious.

To Ruby, Raygen was the source of all her hope. For years, she had trusted him, believed in him. He alone had never betrayed her. Edward knew she would trust Raygen in an instant over himself. Why, she and Edward had been fighting ever since they met.

"Ruby, please deal with him," Raygen said, ducking out

into the hall. He no longer seemed interested in going out the cellar exit. He headed for the back of the mansion.

"Wait, you!" Edward began to chase after him, but in that moment, a fist swept by his hair.

"I won't let you go, Edward!"

"You're worse than Raygen in some ways, you know that?" Edward said wryly, glancing at the fist that had nearly caught him on the cheek.

"Oh, and you're some kind of saint?" Ruby shot back, glaring at Edward.

The two stood staring at each other, faces inches apart. Then, almost without warning, both leapt back at the same time.

"You dummy—won't you listen to what your Raygen's been up to?"

"What? The weapons? I know about that!"

Ruby flew into arm's reach of Edward with surprising speed and charged toward Edward's jaw with her right fist.

"Whoa!" Edward dodged the fist and barely knocked aside the foot that came for his stomach with his left hand.

Which was exactly what Ruby had planned, for as soon as she got her right leg back on the ground, she twisted. Her left leg drew an arc through the air, coming straight at Edward.

"I see why they call you the toughest in town . . . but you're still not tough enough!"

Edward crouched, letting Ruby's circle kick sweep over his head. He grabbed her spinning arm and used her momentum to flip her onto the ground.

"Ow!"

"You need some more practice," Edward said, shaking his head.

"That's my line!" she spat back at him.

With her shoulder pressed to the ground, Ruby turned her head to glare at Edward.

Her eyes held no trace of defeat, and with more strength than Edward gave her credit for, she sprang to her feet.

"Okay, you are strong. But I can't place the fighting style. An original?" asked Edward as he brushed away her fists.

"You bet. I've been training daily. See, I hate to lose."

"Hate to lose to whom, I wonder?"

Ruby's hand stopped for the briefest of moments.

"Are you protecting the town . . . or Raygen?"

"Both!" shouted Ruby, charging.

Ruby's arm swung in a fierce punch, but Edward stopped it in midair.

"Listen to me! This Raygen you're so dedicated to protecting? In this town you care about? He's selling the people like meat at a market."

Ruby was unimpressed. She snorted. "Who would believe that?"

Apparently, she believed Raygen. In her eyes, Edward was merely trying to blame him for crimes he didn't commit. The accusation washed right over her.

But Edward's next words made her body go rigid and her

face go pale. "The ones he can use, he keeps close to him as his loyal slaves. The ones who can work, he puts to work mining his fortune. The criminals, he sells to the military, and the ones he has no use for at all, he sells to anyone who's buying. Raygen doesn't think of the people in this town as human beings. You know those letters you carry out every once in a while? That's Raygen selling out your neighbors to the military!"

"Th-that's a lie! Raygen takes in people with no place to go! He would never sell . . ."

"Three days ago. And on the twelfth and twenty-sixth of last month. And the sixteenth of the month before that!"

Ruby's face grew more and more pale as Edward spoke.

"He's using those letters. You're the one who sent them out, right? Up on the third floor here, I've got the broker who tried to buy Leaf. Do you see now?"

Edward let go of Ruby's fist. Ruby took a few uncertain steps back and collapsed to the floor. "It's a lie. It has to be a lie . . ." she repeated desperately.

But how could Edward, whom she had only met a few days before, know about the letters she had sent out months ago? And Edward's calm, serious composure—totally unlike the Edward that had fought with her before—made his words hard to ignore.

Everything Ruby saw told her that he was telling the truth.

Just then there was a loud grinding noise.

"What's that?"

The sound came from outside.

Edward whirled around, but Ruby did not let him go.

"Don't you get it yet?!" Edward said. He was still trying to turn away, but his trapped arm was wrapped around his neck, holding him fast.

"Yeah . . . But even if that's true, Mr. Raygen saved me!"

Edward heard it in her voice: Ruby half understood now, yet still she resisted. She couldn't entirely escape Raygen's spell. She whirled and caught a punch directly in her solar plexus.

"Wake up, Ruby!"

They heard the grinding sound once again.

Edward dropped to his knees and clapped his hands together. Then he put his hands on the floor.

An incredible amount of light and electricity filled the mansion, the mansion shook, and the door to the back folded into the wall, leaving a giant hole.

Behind was the sluice gate with its massive wooden handle. The giant handle managed the flow of water, so big it took two hands to turn it. The handle screeched.

Raygen, his eyes mad, threw all his strength into pushing the handle.

"If I'm going to be caught, I'm taking all of you with me!"

The water flowing to the aboveground channel began to drop. At the same time, the sound of water flowing underground grew to a deafening roar.

Edward jumped through the hole, fashioning his right arm into a pole, and brought it down toward Raygen.

"Stop that!"

Raygen lifted his hand from the handle and dropped to his knees, pressing his hands to the ground.

Edward looked down to see an alchemical circle drawn on the earth.

There was a flash of alchemical light, and the ground surged. Knowing what was coming, Edward dodged to the side with ease. The earthen spike slammed into the mansion, driving deep cracks into the wall from beneath.

Raygen fired off another shot. This time, the ground buckled and hollowed out beneath him. Raygen's alchemy was energetic, uncontrolled, but its sheer destructive power impressed Edward.

Walls crumbled, and the roof of the mansion flew up and back.

"Ruby!" Edward turned to look for her—she had still been in the mansion.

Luckily, thanks to the sheer power of Raygen's alchemy, the broken splinters of wood and clay tiles launched high into the air, and Ruby lay trembling on the floor of the now-roofless mansion, unharmed.

"You've gone too far!"

Raygen unleashed the full might of his alchemy, unconcerned even about Ruby's well-being. Ruby alone had stayed true to him until the very end, but now, he cared not one whit if she was caught in the wreckage. He truly wanted to take all of Wisteria and its people out with him. Edward felt himself fill with anger. He slapped his hands together and touched the ground.

Alchemical light flared, and Raygen tensed, but nothing happened. Then, the cliff a short distance from the sluice gate buckled and warped, protruding in a sharp stone spike that thrust at Raygen.

Raygen raised another spike of earth with his alchemical circle, directing it toward the stone shaft. Raygen's spike struck from directly below, shattering Edward's and raining chunks of stone and earth down on Raygen's head.

Raygen shielded his eyes from the dust and gravel. When he looked up again, Edward's fist was coming right at his face.

FROM A SHORT DISTANCE AWAY, Ruby watched as Edward struggled to turn back the sluice gate handle. Raygen lay unconscious behind him.

She had heard the truth from Edward. She had heard Raygen's maniacal laughter as he sought to destroy the town he had built. She had seen the battle before her eyes.

Ruby sat crouched on her hands and knees, her face forward, staring in mute horror.

Everything she had believed in lay in ruin before her eyes.

"I don't want to be weak, I don't want to be weak . . ." Ruby repeated the phrase over and over. It was the only thing she could hold on to.

These words had guided her every day since she had met Raygen. She had repeated these words whenever she felt doubt. Every time she said them, she felt brave again.

But now, those words left her empty.

"I don't want to be weak. I want to be happy," she repeated. Ruby remembered what Alphonse had told her sitting on the bridge over the waterway. It seemed like so long ago now. She heard his gentle, melancholy voice again in her heart.

If you cut away everyone who disagrees with you, don't you know what you will become in the end? There will be no one left!

Ruby hugged the ground.

Her stomach hurt from Edward's punch. A deep despair consumed her. Her eyes clouded, and everything was blurry. When she looked down, a teardrop fell on the back of her hand. A cold night breeze blew, running over her body.

She moaned, and with every sob, the tears in her eyes ran down her cheeks.

A single flower petal fell on her wet hand. A white petal, like the ones from the flowers that had grown in her hometown—hers and Leaf's.

She looked at the petal. Leaf had given those flowers to her. He had told her to open her eyes. Now that she had, she realized something. It was her favorite color of flower.

Ruby grabbed the petal firmly in her hand.

"I don't want to be weak. I want to be happy. I have to be strong to be happy! I have to look forward. I have to be better than anyone else! I can't look back, but . . ."

She lifted her eyes.

In the night sky, white petals came fluttering down, dancing on the cool night air.

"But what's the point of being the best if you're the only person left?"

Ruby stood up, turning her eyes back to Edward. She saw him struggling to turn back the handle, fighting with all his strength to save Wisteria. And then behind him, she saw Raygen rise to his knees and place his hands on the earth.

Licking the blood from a cut on his lip, Raygen glowered at Edward. His hands flashed with light, and the earth buckled.

"You never should have turned your back on me!"

The ground swelled like boiling water. A surge ripped across the dirt, sending rocks flying, all the way to Edward. The ground before Edward rose.

"You don't know when to give up!"

Edward let go of the handle and pressed his hands together. Dropping to his knees, he touched the ground, drawing up a wall in front of him. Then he kicked the wall with all his strength.

The ground shook, and the wall toppled onto the swollen earth. A great cloud of dust rose.

But in the little time that he took to fight Raygen, water continued to flood the underground passages. He could waste no more time fighting. Raygen knew this. He was trying to stall, to keep Edward from redirecting the water.

Edward hestitated, unsure of what to do. The night wind swept away the rising cloud of dust.

"You should never have turned your back on me, either!" shouted Ruby in a shrill voice.

Raygen spun and faced Ruby. Her eyes shone with a strong will, the will of one who has chosen to walk her own path at last.

Edward watched Ruby's foot fly into Raygen's chest. In the next instant, Raygen flew several feet across the floor and slumped to the ground, unconscious.

"Ruby, you—"

Edward ran to the sluice gate without giving Raygen another glance.

"What?!"

Ruby put her hands on the handle. She glared at Edward as she leaned into it.

"No, I'm glad. I needed a lost cause like you to see the light, or I wouldn't have felt like I'd made a difference," Edward said, even though it would have sufficed for him to say he was glad.

"Yes, I did open my eyes . . . and it's all thanks to Alphonse and Leaf," she replied.

"What?! I helped too!"

"You're lame. Who needs your help?!"

The two exchanged insults and barbs as they had the first time they met, but they soon stopped and laughed.

"Let's give this a rest. Alphonse isn't here to stop it for us," Ruby said.

"Yeah, I could go on like this forever." The two grabbed the handle and pulled at it as hard as they could. And the handle began to turn.

IN THE UNDERGROUND WATERWAY, Alphonse, the townspeople, and the security guards screamed as the rushing water climbed higher around them. They pressed deeper into the caverns as fast as they could.

"Why is all this water coming down here? This is bad!" Alphonse said, turning to look behind them.

The footpath on either side of the waterway had already flooded. Everyone pushed downstream, the water lapping at their knees.

Even though they carried lamps, their feet were in darkness, and with the water churning around their legs, it was difficult to walk.

The waterway path sloped downward slightly. If more water came in and the flow increased, they wouldn't be able to walk down the waterway—they would be washed away.

Leaf walked with his arm looped around Kett's waist, helping him keep his balance on the flooded path. Leaf shouted over the sound of rushing water and the roaring wind as the rising waters forced out the tunnel's air. "Somebody must have switched the sluice gate to redirect more water this way!"

"We should go back . . ." Alphonse began. Next to him, Ivans grabbed on to Alphonse's arm.

"If somebody's doing this on purpose, there's no way you'll make it back in time. The water will rise too swiftly. We should keep going forward."

Alphonse called ahead to the front of the line. "Neil!"

The lantern light swayed, and he heard Neil call out. "Eh?"

"How much farther is it?"

"Just a little more, I think!"

Leaf stretched as high as he could and looked ahead. "We're past the factory where they raise the stones. We should be nearing the downstream part of town soon."

Then they heard Neil's voice from the front.

"I found something!"

"Have we made it?" But drowning out that voice came the tremendous sound of crashing water behind them.

"Everyone, hold on!" Alphonse shouted. He grabbed the nearby Leaf, Kett, and Ivans in his metal arms. Part of the tunnel behind them must have collapsed. A new surge of water came rushing in, carrying sand and gravel with it.

Screams echoed throughout the tunnel.

The wooden paths at either side of the waterway could not hold much longer. Alphonse called out again. "Everyone, just a little farther! Hold on!"

After a short distance, they came to a large open space.

"What is this?!" one of the townsfolk shouted.

The tunnel had opened up suddenly into a wide hall. The waterway was supposed to curve here and rejoin the water that ran through the village before going farther underground. There was supposed to be a door here and a mining tunnel going south.

But here in this large space, the water channel simply vanished. Instead, there was a large pond, deep enough to go up past their ankles. The water level was no longer rising, but the townspeople took no comfort from this fact.

The passageway that was supposed to take them out of here was nowhere to be seen. It was just a vast cavern.

"Are you sure we're in the right place?" Neil asked Leaf.

"We are. If you go downstream, there should be a wide-open area connected to the waterway. We were supposed to take the mining tunnel farthest to the right to get out of here."

"You don't sound too certain," somebody in the crowd said.

"This is revenge, isn't it? You're getting even with us all for picking on you," said another.

"He would never do that," Alphonse said, defending Leaf. "Look at that wall: see those layers of rock? That means these caverns aren't too stable, especially not when those layers have absorbed so much water. I'll bet the explosives those bandits used must have made a section of the tunnel collapse. It's not Leaf's fault."

Alphonse shone his lantern on the wall opposite the cavern's entrance.

At last he spotted it: a place where the wall had fallen down. Gravel created a gentle slope that had buried their only other exit from the tunnel.

"So what do we do now?" somebody asked. "If we had just left earlier, we wouldn't be stuck here . . . " The man pointed his finger accusingly at Neil.

"You're the one who closed off the mansion entrance!"

"You want to blame us?!" Neil barked back. "You old folks are slowing us down! You can't keep up the pace!"

"Please, we don't have time for this," Alphonse said, stepping between the men.

But fatigue and fear at finding this dead end had finally brought the townspeople's unhappiness boiling to a head.

"You always blame us for everything in this town!"

"I bet you know another way out, don't you!"

"Tell us!"

As the fighting began, several men dropped their lanterns into the water. They went out with a hiss. Just before one of the lanterns went out, its light flickered against the surface of the water. In that brief flash, Leaf saw something white floating in the water.

"What's this?" Leaf reached out to pick it up. "One of my flowers! How did that get in here?" He looked up into the darkness of the cavern. Another white petal fell from somewhere above.

"Everyone!" Leaf shouted. "Your lamps! Turn off your lamps!"

The fighting men, surprised to hear the normally soft-spoken Leaf shouting, stopped arguing, and the angry crowd fell silent.

"I said turn off your lamps!"

Leaf grabbed a lamp from a man and doused its flame.

"But how will we see?"

"Don't worry about it! Please, trust me!"

Cowed by his insistence, the townspeople put out their lamps one by one. When the last lamp was extinguished, a pale beam of light could be seen arcing through the room.

"What's that light?"

"It's the moon!" Leaf turned back and looked at everyone. "There must be a hole in the ceiling!"

"I see! The collapse must have broken clean through to the surface! If we climb up here, we can get to the top of the cliff!" said Alphonse.

The townspeople looked at each other, uncertain, and remained where they stood. They knew that the wet, steep slope would be no easy climb.

But Leaf did not hesitate. "Let's go! It might be tough, but if we work together, we can make it out! I know it!"

Neil took a step forward and planted his foot at the base of the slope. "Come on, Kett," he said, stretching his hand out behind him. "Let's get out of here. I'll help you. We'll get out together."

Kett sat in the water, holding his injured leg. He looked at Neil for only a moment before reaching out and taking Neil's hand.

"Let's go."

"Neil . . ." Alphonse said.

Neil snorted. "Hey, I watch out for my own." He supported Kett's frail body with a firm but gentle grip.

"You won't be able to get them all up yourself," another man said, walking over to Ivans. "I'll help you up. Let's go." It was the same man who had grabbed Ivans by the collar during the almost-fight the other day.

"I'll carry this one. Hey, you help too."

Another man carrying a child called out to the people downstream. Another person carried the woman from the restaurant. Another carried the wounded security guard. One by one, the people of Wisteria joined hands to climb the steep slope.

"We'll all go together, Leaf!" Leaf wiped a tear from his eye and nodded.

The slope was steeper than any of them had imagined. Wet earth dirtied their hands, making their grips slick against the damp rock, and their footholds seemed always on the verge of crumbling. But still, the people of Wisteria helped one another and climbed slowly higher.

"Help!"

A child right above Leaf slipped. Leaf, climbing at the bottom, reached out a hand.

"Watch out!"

He held the kid who was about to fall and pressed him against the slope. But the added weight was too much. Leaf's feet began to slip.

"Yipes!"

"Leaf!" Somebody shouted for help, but Leaf had already begun to tumble off the slope.

"Gotcha!" Edward said with a smile in his voice. He had caught Leaf by the collar just as Leaf's feet gave out.

"Edward?!"

"You watch yourself, Leaf!" said Ruby, climbing at Edward's side. They had succeeded in closing the sluice gate and raced to catch up with the others. Now, they all made their way up the steep slope together.

"Ed!"

Edward flashed a smile at his brother climbing nearby and he too resumed the brutal climb.

"Just a little farther. Let's do this!"

"You got it."

The moonlit gap in the cavern roof seemed close enough to touch.

THE TOP OF THE CLIFF shone in the moonlight, casting a supernatural glow on Leaf's pale white flowers. They spread out in a vast field before the escapees from Wisteria.

At the top of the cliff on the other side of the valley, military teams from the nearest bases were rounding up the bandits trying to escape with the jewels. Among the people taken away in chains stood a familiar man with silver hair.

Perhaps they all understood what had happened, for none of the people of Wisteria felt the need to talk. They stood silently and watched as the man they had respected, the man they had vowed to follow forever, was led away, no better than the bandits who had destroyed the only home they had.

The wind blew, and the flowers danced in the desert breeze. White petals fluttered down on the broken town of Wisteria.

"It's going to be okay," Ruby said. "We can build it all again. Everything will be okay. If we all work together, we can do anything."

"Ruby . . ."

Leaf quietly grabbed Ruby's hand. Ruby squeezed it back.

They had lost the one they believed in, and the town they had lived in was destroyed, but they weren't alone.

The sky in the east grew gradually lighter. Night fell away as the new day dawned. Ruby and Leaf looked up from the ruins of Wisteria to face the rising sun. Neil, Ivans, and the others all looked in the same direction, the rosy light of dawn casting a warm glow on their faces. Some seemed sad, others angry, but all were filled with the determination to rebuild what they had once possessed.

They had worked only for profit. They had been divided. Sometimes, they had even fought, but now they knew that kindness could not be measured in money, and true success came only by working together. They no longer had a need for any law of equivalent exchange.

"I'm glad we came here, Ed."

"Same here."

Before long, the dazzling rays of the morning sun fell on all the people of Wisteria.

"TAKE CARE of yourself," Ruby told Edward and Alphonse.

"Thanks."

The sun shone high in the sky, and at the top of the cliff under the cloudless blue, Edward and Alphonse prepared to leave on their next journey.

"Ruby, Leaf, hang in there. I know it will be hard, but you can make it work."

"We'll be fine," Ruby said, looking down at the town with Leaf.

Neil and the others had spent most of the day putting out fires throughout the town. Ivans cared for the wounded, while the others cleared away the rubble of fallen houses and the ruined refinery. The town was alive with activity.

"We'll be busy for a while, I think. We won't have any time to be sad. And without as many people living here, it's going to be hard. But we'll do what we can."

"Not as many people? Why?"

"A lot of people living in Wisteria had prices on their heads. They've all turned themselves in to the military."

"Really . . ."

"They'll be back, though. Once they've done their time, they've promised to come back."

That too was a choice.

Freed from Raygen's sway, the people of Wisteria no longer had one single voice to guide them. Now, they thought for themselves. Now, they chose their own paths.

"Thank you so much. I'm glad I met you," Ruby said to Alphonse, smiling. "Promise you'll come again soon, Alphonse."

"You bet. Next time I want to see everyone in town smiling. I'll be sure to visit."

"Yes. You'll have to let us take good care of you when you do, Alphonse."

"Hey, there are two of us here, you know!" Edward said, glaring at Ruby.

"What, you want to come back too?"

"Who would want to go see a wretched little brat like you?!"

"Wretched? You're the one who's wretched! I know, you're still jealous because I took away your little brother!"

"Jealous?! Who's jealous?!"

"You know, you're a lot alike, the two of you," Leaf said,

looking at Edward and Ruby.

"No way!" the two yelled as one.

"Please, please," Alphonse said, trying to stop the endless disputes. "Can't you get along, just this once?"

"Not a chance. Al, we're leaving!" Edward said, snorting. He turned and walked off.

"Good-bye, Ruby, Leaf," Alphonse said, saying his final farewells. He was about to run off to catch up with his brother, when he heard Ruby's voice.

"Alphonse?"

"Huh?"

Alphonse heard a light, wet, kissing sound.

"Let me know if you ever need a fiancée again," Ruby said, standing on her tiptoes, her lips still touching Alphonse's cheek.

"Whaaaa?!"

Alphonse, flustered, stepped back and placed a hand on his cheek. Ruby began to laugh, a flower in full bloom.

"I'll be waiting!"

"R-Ruby?!" Alphonse gaped, his voice shifting up a full octave. Even though his cheek couldn't feel anything, he could swear it was burning.

Not knowing what to do or what to say, Alphonse stood flustered and dumbstruck. Edward called out from far ahead.

"Al, what're you doing!? We're leaving!"

"R-right! Coming! So, uh, 'bye."

"'Bye."

"Take care."

Alphonse waved to Ruby and Leaf one final time and ran after Edward. Edward looked at Alphonse, who seemed unusually agitated as they walked.

"What were you talking about?"

"Oh, n-nothing."

From behind them in the distance came Ruby's loud voice. "Alphonse, Edward, thank you so much!"

Edward was startled a moment. Then, he smiled and, without turning around, waved his hand.

TWO WEEKS LATER.

"Colonel, telephone for you."

Roy was in a meeting at Eastern Command when Fuery interrupted him.

Roy scowled. "I'm in a meeting. Can't this wait?"

"It's from General Hakuro in New Optain."

Roy made a face like he'd eaten something bitter. He rose from his chair and turned to the others in the meeting room. "Just read the reports we have until I get back." With that, he went to the nearest phone.

"He better not have more work for me. I thought I gained some credit with that affair in Wisteria the other day."

Roy scratched his neck and picked up the phone. "Thanks for waiting."

"Colonel Mustang, thanks for your hard work the other day."

"Not at all, sir."

Maybe he was calling to thank him, thought Roy, then Hakuro went on. "I was looking at this observation report you sent in. It was quite well done, overall. There's a lot of good information in here for us."

Most of what Hakuro now praised was Havoc and Breda's work. Roy had signed off on it, so he knew it was good stuff.

"But there was a problem with one page."

Roy knew immediately that it was the page Edward had written. But Roy kept his cool. He knew better than to expect that Edward's report would be well written or even legible. Still, he figured that Edward's experience would provide valuable insight, so he assigned the final evaluation to Edward. Thanks to his prior research and his own involvement in the arrests at Wisteria, Roy knew, at least, what Havoc and Breda had written. He assumed he could fake any answers he didn't have firsthand.

"I'm sorry, you're speaking about Wisteria, right?"

"Yes."

"Well, there had been an incident, sir. I couldn't write well . . ."

"So it seems."

"Which part had a problem? The bit about the town's finances? Or the report on the guards?" Roy fished for some hint of where the problem lay.

But Hakuro didn't take the bait. In fact, he seemed confused.

"Colonel Mustang, are we talking about the same thing? I'm not entirely sure you understand the problem."

"What do you mean?" Now it was Roy's turn to be confused.

"Have you forgotten what you wrote? Let me refresh your memory: 'Regarding Wisteria, please look forward to a full report, coming soon!' That's all. What's the meaning of this?"

Roy fell silent.

"You did write this, didn't you?"

He couldn't admit that he hadn't. Nor could he own up to who *had* written those words. If he did, his own negligence would reflect poorly on his standing with Central Command. General Hakuro had a reputation for a short temper and little regard for people who slacked in their responsibilities.

"Colonel Mustang? What's the meaning of this? Are you listening to me?"

Roy, uncertain how to answer, sat dumbly holding the phone, praying that, if he just said nothing at all, Hakuro might forget he was there.

Afterword

HELLO, Makoto Inoue here. For this, the third *Fullmetal Alchemist* novel, I went even deeper into the *Fullmetal* world in my head.

I woke to *Fullmetal*. I ate lunch with *Fullmetal*. I watched the sun set with *Fullmetal*. In the bath? *Fullmetal!* In bed? *Fullmetal! Fullmetal* all the time, 24/7! Even in my dreams . . . *Fullmetal!* And, of course, when I went to the bathroom, well . . . you get the idea. But back to the point, this installment of *Fullmetal Alchemist* was enough to make me forget everything else! In the end, this novel I wrote carves out its own little chunk of the *Fullmetal* world. I hope everyone who reads it can forget herself (or himself!) and enter a *Fullmetal* world all her (or his!) own. I hope when you do reach that *Fullmetal* moment of your own, you'll shout with me, "Hey! That right there is what *Fullmetal*'s all about!" [musical note] If you're not shouting and screaming . . . sorry.

AFTERWORD

MANY PEOPLE helped me this time, same as before.

First and foremost, I must thank Arakawa-sensei. Though she was very busy, she helped me with characterization. I loved every minute working with her. I'm sure you're still busy, Arakawa-sensei, so be sure to take care of yourself.

And to Editor Nomoto! I certainly needed your help this time around. Thank you very much.

With all the confusion and mistakes one makes while writing a novel, I'm convinced that the only way I'll ever hold the finished book in my hand is thanks to Nomoto-san's alternating praise and punishment.

Of course, work is fun most of the time, but when you sit there looking at the computer screen forever, sometimes you want to travel—not in a world of your imagination, but in the real world.

That was when I got a perfectly timed telephone call.

Nomoto: Nomoto here. How's work?

Inoue: Oh, uh, it's going. I was just thinking how I'd love a vacation . . .

Nomoto: Of course you would. That's what happens when you stay inside too long.

Inoue: N-Nomoto-san! (You understand how I feel, you really do!)

Nomoto: What about going overseas? For two or three weeks?

Inoue: Two or three weeks!? But I'm busy . . .

Nomoto: If you're going to go, you should spread your wings and fly far! Once you finish work and can feel good about it, you should have fun! It'll be great.

Inoue: Y-you're right!

Nomoto: Of course! Just keep working, visions of a cottage in some foreign land floating in your head.

Inoue: Right! (I can see the blue sea waters already!)

THEN, right before work was finished . . . (The important part is right before, not right after.)

Nomoto: Good work! Just got some last checking left to do!

Inoue: Yep. Once this is done, I'm thinking of going on a trip.

Nomoto: Ah! Right. Speaking of which, are you free next week?

Inoue: Uh . . . yes. Why?

Nomoto: Great! Actually, I was thinking I wanted to have a meeting with you about the next job!

Inoue: Uh . . . Or a beach, maybe?

Nomoto: Oh, that's right! You said something about wanting to visit the sea before. You should go after your next job is finished, really! Nothing beats taking a little trip right after a big job!

Inoue: Oh . . . right . . .

Nomoto: Of course! Now, back to work, visions of a Northern European backpacking trek floating through your head!

Inoue: Uh . . . right. (I can see the rugged coast of Finland already!)

LESS PRAISE and punishment . . . and more like incarceration? (I realize only now.)

But I kid! I have nothing but thanks for Nomoto-san. Her pretty voice and pretty face . . . and pretty amazing editorial skills make her great to work with. You've helped me so much, allow me to make it up to you some time!

IT'S ODD, though, how she merely needs to say "Of course!" for me to think reflexively "That's right!" I'm well trained.

HERE'S A LITTLE SOMETHING for those who read the afterword in volume 2. Remember how I actually had to buy a new computer?

I'm not even a true Action Novelist yet, so why?! Is it so wrong to bang at one's keyboard with all one's might?! (Of course!)

To all those intending to become "Action Novelists," go easy on your keyboard. To those who want to use their computer lovingly for a long time, I recommend becoming a "Romance Novelist." Yes, keyboards are meant to be handled the way one handles fine glasswork, with a gentle touch. And don't forget the rose-scented perfume and bubbles!

IN CLOSING, let me thank each and every person who read this book! Thanks!

—MAKOTO INOUE

AFTERWORD (kinda)

What does one write in an afterword, anyway?
Hello everyone, Arakawa here. Many thanks for
picking up this *Fullmetal Alchemist* novel. Look at
that! We've gotten up to volume three! My third
Afterword! What do I write!?

The Phone Call

Pon!*

Hey, that one's mine!

Wait, I'm still looking!

Hurry it up, Colonel.

Um, Colonel!?

I haven't slept...

*Pon = Taking another player's discarded tile to form a hand in Mahjong.

...Done!
Inoue-sensei, Nomoto-san,
good work!
I hope everyone enjoyed it!

Arakawa Hiromu